THE LUCKY RIDE

THE LUCKY RIDE

A NOVEL FULL OF OPPORTUNITY

YASUSHI KITAGAWA

TRANSLATED BY TAKAMI NIEDA

Without limiting the exclusive rights of any author, contributor or the publisher of this publication, any unauthorized use of this publication to train generative artificial intelligence (AI) technologies is expressly prohibited. HarperCollins also exercise their rights under Article 4(3) of the Digital Single Market Directive 2019/790 and expressly reserve this publication from the text and data mining exception.

This is a work of fiction. Names, characters, places, and incidents are products of the author's imagination or are used fictitiously and are not to be construed as real. Any resemblance to actual events, locales, organizations, or persons, living or dead, is entirely coincidental.

THE LUCKY RIDE copyright © 2019 by Kitagawa Yasushi. English translation copyright © 2025 by Takami Nieda. All rights reserved. Printed in Malaysia. No part of this book may be used or reproduced in any manner whatsoever without written permission except in the case of brief quotations embodied in critical articles and reviews. For information, address HarperCollins Publishers, 195 Broadway, New York, NY 10007. In Europe, HarperCollins Publishers, Macken House, 39/40 Mayor Street Upper, Dublin 1, D01 C9W8, Ireland.

HarperCollins books may be purchased for educational, business, or sales promotional use. For information, please email the Special Markets Department at SPsales@harpercollins.com.

Originally published as 運転者 未来を変える過去からの使者 in Japan in 2019 by Discovery 21. English edition published by arrangement with Discovery 21, Inc., through Japan Creative Agency Inc., Tokyo

harpercollins.com

FIRST HARPERONE PAPERBACK PUBLISHED IN 2025

Designed by Yvonne Chan

Library of Congress Cataloging-in-Publication Data has been applied for.

ISBN 978-0-06-337624-3

25 26 27 28 29 PCA 10 9 8 7 6 5 4 3 2 1

THE LUCKY RIDE

PROLOGUE

You've had a phenomenal year.

Thank you.

I understand you write your own music and lyrics. When did you decide to pursue a career in the music industry?

I'm a bit of a late bloomer. My father brought home a guitar when I was in junior high school . . .

zzzt . . .

> Grounded out with a man on in his last at bat. I'm sure he'd like to get a hit here to bring the runner home. What do you think goes through a batter's mind in this situation?

THE TAXI DRIVER CHANGED THE RADIO STATION to the baseball broadcast perhaps out of consideration for Shuichi sitting in the back seat. He appeared to be around Shuichi's age.

"I don't understand the music the kids are listening to these days," the driver muttered, glancing at Shuichi through the rearview mirror.

"Yeah, right?" Shuichi answered, pushing a smile. "But I think I'd rather listen to the music program over the game."

"Right, sorry." The driver switched the station again.

And your father is a consultant of some kind?

A financial planner, yes.

Sounds like he played a prominent role in shaping who you are today. Let's talk about the new release. The single is "TAXI," off the album Life Is Beautiful, *which dropped on the twentieth of this month. Tell us more about it.*

One day, I took a ride in a rather peculiar taxi, and from that day on, my life was completely transformed. I wrote the song based on that experience.

Okay, let's have a listen. Here now is "TAXI" by Yumeka.

IT WASN'T A SONG SHUICHI HAD HEARD BEFORE, but it sounded pleasant to his ears.

"A peculiar taxi, eh?" he muttered to himself.

Shuichi let slip a smile as a memory he'd not recalled in about a decade came back to him.

DEADLINE

A year seems like an eternity, yet it passes in the blink of an eye.

Everyone feels that way at year's end, but for Shuichi Okada, who had switched careers to life insurance, the passage of a year was fraught with a terror that penetrated to his very core. Each month felt as though he was on the brink of being crushed by that fear.

Although there might have been companies in his industry that offered a fixed salary, Shuichi's company wasn't one of them.

Full commission.

Anyone who'd worked under this compensation model would know his apprehension. For each new contract that was secured, a fixed percentage of the insurance premiums paid by the policyholder went directly to your earnings. Although the percentage varied by company, Shuichi's was fairly generous in this aspect. There was, however, a catch: after the initial one-year period, the percentage dropped significantly. At least, this was how it worked at Shuichi's company. In other words, you could rely on the premiums as income for the first year, but from then on, they became almost negligible. Therefore, you had to secure more contracts before the drop took effect.

Initially, when he thought "there's still six months left," he didn't feel stressed about it, but as the realization of "there's only two months left" dawned on him, he increasingly found himself unable to eat or sleep at night.

SHUICHI GRADUATED FROM A PRIVATE UNIVERSITY in Tokyo that wasn't exactly top-tier. As a result, he struggled mightily during the job hunt, and even after managing to land a position at a company, he bounced around from one job to another before eventually settling at his current one.

His previous job was in sales at a used-car dealership, and it wasn't uncommon for salespeople like Shuichi to transition from selling used cars to selling insurance. While the products were different, both jobs involved dealing with insurance matters, and more importantly, building strong relationships with their clientele. Salespeople knew all manner of details about their clients, such as their family composition as well as the ages of their children. Additionally, understanding what car someone purchased and how provided insight into their income and lifestyle. That kind of information was an asset in this line of work.

The catalyst for the job change was listening to a senior colleague's endless complaints about the used-car dealership and compliments about how wonderful his life was now after changing careers. Indeed, the dealership had more than its fair share of unreasonable aspects.

"If there was a better opportunity, I would jump ship in a heartbeat." That thought was foremost not only in Shuichi's mind but also among many of his colleagues.

Every time they met, the ex–senior colleague tried to persuade him to join his company, saying:

"You can have fun and make easy money as long as you can pull in contracts."

"The good thing about this job is that your earnings depend on your efforts."

"You'd be better off here too."

Shuichi joined the same insurance company only to discover that his colleague had quit shortly thereafter.

After skillfully leveraging past connections to pull in new contracts shortly after changing jobs, even the senior colleague, who initially earned a monthly salary of almost four thousand yen in the first year, faced the challenge of the second year. Less than half a year after Shuichi gave in to temptation and changed careers, the complaints the colleague used to make about the car dealership shifted to complaints about the current company. By the time his income had dwindled to nearly zero, he had mysteriously disappeared.

Though it wasn't clear whether the statistic was based on accurate data, it was said that only 3 percent of insurance agents lasted ten years in the industry. While Shuichi had never considered why that was before starting the job, he now understood the difficulties of surviving a decade in the business.

"GOOD MORNING."

Shuichi barely got the words out before the company president, Takeshi Wakiya, barked, "Okada!" as if he'd been waiting for Shuichi to arrive.

Wakiya always wore a neatly pressed suit and never went without a jacket, even in the increasingly humid summer. Always conscious of his physique, he routinely hit the gym after work to stay in shape. He kept his hair neatly styled and usually wore glasses, though it wasn't clear whether they were for fashion or for their intended purpose.

Wakiya, who was roughly the same age as Shuichi, had founded the company at the age of thirty and steadily expanded its size over the past eighteen years. Currently, there were six employees, including Shuichi. While the company could hardly be considered large, growing a business in this industry from a one-man operation to its current size was no small feat.

The reality was the company's performance was largely thanks to Wakiya. His status as the only member in the company to be named to the Million Dollar Round Table confirmed his skill as a top insurance agent. The MDRT was an international association of life insurance and financial services professionals and required securing a significant number of contracts to earn membership. That the president was able to maintain his membership for ten years running was something Shuichi couldn't even dream of achieving for a single year.

"Yes?" Shuichi answered as he approached Wakiya's desk.

Wakiya glared at him through his glasses. It was a look Shuichi had seen before. It was when one of the contracts he had secured ended up getting canceled. Sensing trouble, he responded again.

"Yes . . . ?"

Wakiya dropped the documents he was holding onto the desk, removed his glasses with his now-free hand, and rubbed the corners of his eyes with the other. After putting his glasses back on, he questioned, "Does the name Saido Seminars ring a bell?"

"Sure . . ." Shuichi's voice was trembling and thin as if it might fade to nothing at any moment.

"They canceled their contracts."

Shuichi was speechless.

Saido Seminars was a cram school that he had stumbled upon ten months ago. As luck would have it, the head teacher, Yuto Asakura, had been interested in hearing Shuichi's pitch from the beginning and had signed up almost immediately.

As it happened, Asakura had recently gotten married, and he and his wife were expecting a child. The life change prompted him to consider purchasing life insurance. The opportunity couldn't have come at a better time for Shuichi.

The school was filled with young teachers, and given that the head teacher didn't have life insurance, it stood to reason no one else did either. Encouraged by the head teacher's casual suggestion that the others should consider getting insurance too, a chorus of "me too" spread quickly through the school, and before Shuichi knew it, he had twenty applications in just two months.

This turn of luck had truly saved Shuichi. Without it, he might not have continued at his job, considering the challenges he faced in securing contracts at the time.

"Who . . . canceled?" Shuichi finally asked, his dry throat barely managing to get out the words.

Wakiya expelled a long sigh and shook his head. "All of them."

Shuichi's mind went blank. Twenty policies canceled

within a year of issuance! Not only would the insurance premiums for the upcoming month be deducted from his next month's salary, but he would also have to refund the insurance premiums paid over the past ten months to the company. Even a quick mental calculation told him that would amount to a staggering sum.

That's it. I'm finished.

On the wall behind Wakiya's desk hung a framed piece of calligraphy.

It was a saying, written in someone's hand, that Wakiya was rather fond of.

Stay positive, and laugh more than anyone else.

Every time Wakiya would talk about the virtue of "staying positive" in morning meetings, Shuichi, a natural pessimist, would think, *If staying positive were so easy, no one would have to struggle in life.* He never said it out loud, of course.

Given that he struggled to maintain a bright outlook under normal circumstances, there was no way he could see this grim situation positively. And it was certainly nothing to laugh about.

"Well, you're not accomplishing anything by just standing there," Wakiya said to Shuichi, who was frozen in bewilderment.

Shuichi snapped back to reality.

"R-right, I'll go to Saido Seminars immediately," he said weakly.

As Shuichi left the office he had only just arrived at, the mood of his colleagues seemed to suggest, *It won't be long before he's gone.*

Paying a visit to the cram school wouldn't change anything. Everyone knew that. Not to mention, the school wouldn't even be open at this early hour. Yet none of his colleagues stopped him from leaving.

"I FEEL TERRIBLE ABOUT THIS, OKADA-SAN, I REALLY do. But she's the mother of one of our students," said Asakura awkwardly.

Gaggles of junior high school students greeted Asakura as they headed to their classrooms. He responded to each student with a "hello," his attention focused more on them than on Shuichi as they conversed.

It was likely nearing the start of class as teachers nearby began to stir. Some of them, having canceled their insurance, cast sidelong glances toward them, seemingly curious about their conversation.

"Still, I wish you'd at least consulted me about it."

"We didn't have time. You know how aggressive some of the saleswomen can be."

Of course, he knew. Shuichi had been in this job for three years and had watched housewives with less experience in the business secure contract after contract, outperforming him. The assertiveness these women showed once they got on a roll was something Shuichi wasn't capable of imitating. In fact, although his daughter attended a different cram school, he couldn't bring himself to approach her teachers with a sales pitch.

"Besides, our insurance premiums are quite a bit lower. We're saving fourteen thousand yen compared to staying with you."

"But you—" Shuichi began to protest but stopped himself short. He caught himself boiling with anger, yet saying more in this state wouldn't lead to anything productive. He didn't come to argue.

Shuichi could have offered a cheaper insurance plan but had deliberately refrained from doing so out of consideration for Asakura's future and his coverage needs. Besides, it was Asakura who had rejected a cheaper option, expressing his preference for a savings plan over a fixed plan. Therefore, the contract he had agreed to should have been one he was satisfied with.

If Shuichi heard the price point and the name of the competing company, he could easily figure out the exact pitch the agent used to persuade Asakura to switch, as well as the type of insurance he switched to. That was why he felt the strong urge to say something. But since he had always stuck to a policy of not bad-mouthing the competition, he elected to hold his tongue.

"If you've reconsidered your insurance needs, I'm certain we can offer a more affordable option—"

Frowning, Asakura cut him off. "I'm sorry, Okada-san. I have to go to class. Anyway, we already made the switch, and I don't intend to switch back. We value our relationships too, and we can't afford to sever ties with the parent of one of our students. You understand. I'm sorry, but I'm afraid the situation is the same for the other teachers. We appreciate everything you've done for us."

He then bowed his head, as if appealing for understanding, and stood up from his seat.

Shuichi thought about insisting once more but decided against it. Despite leaving the office to escape Wakiya's reprimand, he knew from the outset that the situation was hopeless. He understood that his dropping into the school after they'd canceled their insurance wouldn't lead to them saying, "Well, in that case, we'll switch back!"

Doing his utmost to calm himself, Shuichi forced a smile across his face. "I understand. It's unfortunate, but I appreciate your business. If there's anything that I can help you with in the future, please don't hesitate to contact me." He knew there likely wouldn't be a next time, and if there were, the chances of him still being in this job were slim.

A hint of relief floated across Asakura's face.

ONCE SHUICHI WAS OUTSIDE THE SCHOOL, HE LET out a deep sigh.

The cell phone in his chest pocket was vibrating. He assumed it would be Wakiya, but it was his wife, Yuko. He answered the phone, still roiling with frustration.

"What is it? I'm working."

Yuko began, regardless, "You didn't forget, did you? We have a meeting today at school about Yumeka."

Shuichi detected a hint of irritation in her voice. He hastily glanced at his watch. It had completely slipped his mind that she had asked him to attend the meeting at Yumeka's school, and he lied in the spur of the moment.

"I know, I know, but I'm a little busy right now. I can't just leave in the middle of work."

"Don't you think I know that? If you couldn't make it, I wish you would have told me, that's all. I can go alone."

Shuichi clicked his tongue softly, careful not to be heard on the other end. If that was her plan, she should have told him so from the beginning instead of asking him to go along.

"Sure, go listen to what they have to say."

"Okay. Oh, and did you send payment for our trip?"

Shuichi faltered for an answer. "Not . . . yet."

"Will you make sure to do it? If we don't pay by next week, our reservation will be canceled."

"Right. By the way . . ."

"Yeah?"

"Nah, it's nothing. Anyway, thanks for going."

Just before he ended the call, he heard Yuko sigh on the other end.

He felt sorry for Yuko, who had been looking forward to her first visit to Paris, but circumstances had changed since they'd planned the trip. The funds set aside for the trip—actually, an amount several times more than that—had to be returned to the company.

The thought of having to explain this to her weighed heavily on his heart.

He had an inkling of what the meeting might be about. His daughter, Yumeka, had stopped going to school shortly after the new semester had begun.

Shuichi glanced at his watch again. If he took a taxi, he would likely arrive about twenty minutes late. He might still be able to make a brief appearance. He stopped alongside the street and watched the flow of traffic. Just then, he spotted a taxi coming from about a hundred meters behind him. He raised his hand to flag it down, but it turned left at the intersection just before reaching him.

He sucked his teeth.

He decided to walk to a busier road and make a call on the way. He had noticed an incoming call notification when he answered Yuko's call earlier. The call was from his mother, Tamiko, who lived alone in the countryside.

His mother rarely called unless she had a very good reason. Though he couldn't fathom what it might be, he had a feeling it wasn't good news.

Leaving the uncertainty about the purpose of the call hanging unsettled him. Shuichi tapped on the screen and called his mother.

The ringtone rang for a while, but that was nothing unusual.

Given the time of day, she was probably in the

kitchen making herself dinner. Shuichi called up a mental picture of the layout of his childhood home.

She was probably just noticing the phone ringing, wiping her hands on the towel hanging on the cabinet beneath the sink, and walking toward the phone. Recently, she had been complaining about her knees, so it would take some time for her to reach it.

As he waited at a red light, Shuichi noticed the people around him beginning to cross the street, indicating the pedestrian light had turned green.

When he was about halfway across the crosswalk, his mother, Tamiko, finally answered the phone.

"Hello, Okada residence."

As times changed, so, too, did social norms. When Shuichi was a child, his mother taught him that it was proper etiquette to clearly state one's family name when answering the phone. However, nowadays, whenever he made a sales call to a residence, no one ever identified themselves upon answering the phone. The caller's number was displayed, so it wasn't necessary to provide personal information to an unknown person. In some cases, the caller might be trying to scam the elderly into transferring money from their account. That was the era he currently lived in, so the idea of having everyone's home phone numbers listed in a telephone directory might be unthinkable to today's privacy-conscious people.

"Mom, didn't I tell you not to say your name when you don't know who the caller is?"

Now, the child was teaching the parent the opposite of what they had taught them.

"Oh, that's right," Tamiko answered without any hint of remorse.

"What is it, Mom?"

"Oh, I was just wondering if you were coming for a visit this summer."

He hadn't told her yet about their plans to visit Paris during the break. Although, the trip was now in danger of being canceled.

"Summer? We haven't decided on our plans yet. I've been too busy to even think about it. Why do you ask?" Shuichi lied to avoid the bother of explaining.

"Well, only if you can spare some time. You were

in such a rush that we didn't have any time to talk at your father's funeral. I thought we should discuss the future."

Shuichi's father, Masafumi, had died suddenly six months ago. Since he didn't have any known illnesses, his sudden death shocked Shuichi terribly, and it must have been equally shocking for Tamiko.

Starting about one or two years before his father's death, whenever Shuichi called home, his father would always ask, "When are you coming home?" before hanging up. In the end, they never saw each other again.

He should have found a way to go see his father. Had he known his father was ill or doing poorly, he would have done exactly that. But since his father had been in good health, Shuichi ended up not going, citing his busy schedule as an excuse.

The father that Shuichi knew wasn't the type to long for his son's return home. In retrospect, perhaps he'd been worried about seeing Shuichi because he had felt some kind of premonition, although there was no way to confirm that now.

His father died during the busy year-end period, a time when Shuichi was scrambling to secure a few more new contracts. Looking back, he could have taken it easy, as the situation wasn't as dire as it was now. At that moment, however, his focus had been on returning to work as soon as possible, so he rushed to the funeral hall for the wake, stayed overnight at a hotel, attended the funeral service the next morning, and headed straight back to Tokyo.

"Why don't you stay a little longer?" his mother had suggested, but Shuichi responded brusquely, "Things are really tough right now," and quickly left the funeral hall behind.

Shuichi's parents used to run a stationery store inside a shopping arcade in the countryside. The second floor of the shop was the family residence, comprising just a few rooms. Even if it could accommodate Shuichi, it wasn't big enough for Yuko and Yumeka to stay comfortably. Thus, he'd gotten accustomed to staying at a hotel during his visits. Now, he realized he hadn't set foot inside his parents' home on that day.

"The future?" said Shuichi with a hint of annoyance. "What is it? Can we discuss it over the phone?"

Tamiko tried to laugh it off. "I suppose, but . . . not over the phone. Maybe the next time you come . . ."

Shuichi glanced at his watch. He didn't have time for a long conversation, yet Tamiko continued to drone on. Barely able to hide his irritation, he interrupted her rambling.

"Look, I'll talk it over with Yuko and let you know what we decide."

"All right, but you needn't put yourself out. Anyway, how's work? Everything all right?"

"Everything's fine, nothing you need to worry about."

"Just take care of yourself, okay?"

"I know, Mom. I gotta go."

"Oh, sorry."

After he ended the call, his steps were noticeably heavier.

The Okada Stationery Store was initially run by Shuichi's grandmother and passed down to his father when the street was renovated into a shopping district. The store name was changed to Novelty Shop Okada around the time Shuichi entered elementary school. With the addition of character merchandise to their stationery goods, no one recognized it as a stationery store anymore. The shop was always packed with teenagers; after school, the store became so crowded that you could hardly move. The biggest headache for his parents was dealing with shoplifters and complaints from pedestrians due to the number of bicycles blocking the sidewalk outside the store. Unfortunately, there wasn't much they could do about that.

Despite it being a rural town, the shopping arcade was always bustling and the area around the stationery store was said to be the best location for doing business.

Whenever Masafumi had a drink or two, he used to tousle Shuichi's hair and say, "In the future, you can do whatever you want with this place. Doesn't matter what you do here, it'll be profitable."

In those moments, Shuichi had felt a mix of pride

in his father's business savvy and gratitude for the path that his father was paving for him.

Shuichi wasn't the only one to hear these assurances. The other children living in the shopping district also believed that succeeding the family business would be profitable and took pride in their family business. However, many opted to work in the city first before taking over the family business because their parents believed they would be better off experiencing city life. Yet, in their hearts, Shuichi and his childhood friends always held on to the belief that they would succeed in their family business someday.

However, that future never became a reality for any of them.

WAS IT DURING SHUICHI'S COLLEGE DAYS OR AFter he'd started his first job? Shuichi couldn't quite recall, so the phrase "before I knew it" was fitting. Indeed, before he knew it, the shopping arcade had lost its vitality. His father, Masafumi, understood better than anyone that the tides of fortune had shifted, and when Shuichi returned home in the spring of his junior year at university, Masafumi, a drink already in hand, was singing a different tune: "You should try and make it work in the city. You won't have a future coming back to a place like this." To this day, Shuichi couldn't forget the despondent expression on his father's face.

The state of the shopping district after the tide had turned was heartbreaking. Every time Shuichi returned for his annual visit, he found half of the stores shuttered, and hardly any foot traffic. As the number of customers declined, Masafumi's face looked less and less like that of a successful businessman.

Novelty Shop Okada thrived just long enough for Masafumi to send Shuichi to college, but as soon as he landed a job, the customers vanished, bringing an end to the shop's history.

With the closure of Novelty Shop Okada, once bustling with young people, the shopping district became a "shuttered street" in name and reality.

There wasn't an open shop for thirty meters in either direction. It was hard to believe this had once been a place heralded as the prime spot for business. The transformation was so heartbreaking that Shuichi couldn't bear to look. His reluctance to return home was in some part related to his inability to see the arcade in such a state.

Since Masafumi's passing, Shuichi's mother, Tamiko, lived alone on the second floor of the shop. The first floor remained largely unchanged since the shop's closure, and apart from the inventory being cleared out, the shelves and other items remained, frozen in time.

The once ideal environment where Tamiko could fulfill all of her shopping needs within a few minutes' walk in the covered arcade, shielded from rain and snow, had turned into an inconvenience that required her to drive to a distant supermarket in any weather. Moreover, there was an increasing concern about whether she should be driving at her age.

As long as Tamiko remained in good health, the situation was manageable. But if she should fall ill, who would take care of her, and how? There was also the family home to consider. What could be done with a house that, once coveted for its location, no one found desirable? Shuichi didn't have the answers. While he was aware of all the matters that required his attention, he tried his best to avoid them. Besides, he had his hands full managing his own life and simply lacked the bandwidth to think about the family home.

And yet every call he received from his mother reminded him of the reality of the situation. Shuichi knew that like an untreated cavity that worsened over time until it became unbearable, the situation would reach a breaking point. He recognized that he needed to do something before things got worse.

Shuichi let out a deep sigh.

Overwhelmed by troubles at work and concerns about his daughter, his marriage, his mother, and the family home, Shuichi felt utterly lost. It felt as though his head was on the verge of exploding. If he had been alone, he might have been tearing his hair out, but he very well couldn't do that in public.

"Why is all of this happening to me?" Shuichi muttered to himself.

And then . . .

He spotted a taxi approaching. Reflexively, he raised a hand. The vehicle slowed, pulled to the side of the road with its hazards blinking, glided to a halt in front of him, and *ka-chuk!*—the rear door swung open with a pleasant sound.

Shuichi slid into the back seat. The interior had a familiar scent. It was the fragrance of lavender his mother loved and planted in the tiny backyard of their family home.

"Let's see . . ."

Shuichi paused a moment to recall why he'd flagged down the taxi. He had raised his hand without thinking while a million thoughts were occupying his mind.

He caught the driver's eye through the rearview mirror.

The driver, who appeared young enough to be mistaken for a high school student, smiled and said, "Perhaps you'd like to go to your daughter's school first?"

"Right. Yes, the school," Shuichi said hastily, then after a lag, he felt the hairs on his body stand on end.

"Wait, how did you—"

Before Shuichi could finish, the taxi had already started moving.

THE DRIVER

The taxi pulled away and cruised down the road.

Shuichi hadn't given the driver a destination, but they appeared to be headed toward Yumeka's school.

He didn't recognize the driver's face reflected in the rearview mirror.

How did this driver, whom he'd never met, know the location of his daughter's junior high school?

How did he know the junior high school was where he wanted to go?

Shuichi had a mountain of questions, but whenever he was confronted with a strange occurrence, he would never quite know where to start.

He checked the name displayed on the passenger-side dashboard.

Takushi Omakase

The name had to be fake. No driver could possibly have a name like Takushi Omakase, a moniker that literally meant "leave-it-to-me taxi." It must have been some kind of bad joke. The driver just happened to mention "your daughter's school," that's all, Shuichi told himself. Given how the man had simply driven off without knowing the destination, Shuichi expected him to ask, after covering some distance, "So, where to?" The best thing to do was to get out before he got fleeced.

"Stop the car," Shuichi said.

The driver glanced at him through the mirror. "May I ask why?"

"Just stop the car. You're scheming to take me for a ride."

"Huh? What do you mean?" Showing no sign of slowing down, he fixed a look at Shuichi through the mirror. "You're going to miss the school meeting if we don't hurry."

Shuichi started to shout at the driver to stop but caught his breath. "Wait, how do you know that?" He stared suspiciously at the driver's face.

"When you've been at this job as long as I have, you can generally tell where a passenger needs to go," responded the driver. "And you, Okada-san, need to go to Miyabi Junior High School."

This was ridiculous. He had never heard of a taxi driver who knew where a passenger wanted to go without being told, no matter how long they'd been driving. As difficult as it was to believe, the junior high school the driver mentioned was indeed his daughter's school. If he knew that much, what else did he know about Shuichi's life?

On top of that, the driver had called him "Okada-san." After correctly being addressed by his last name, Shuichi had a bad feeling about the young man behind the wheel.

"Who are you?"

"Huh?" said the driver, his voice cracking. He then chuckled and answered, "I'm your driver."

Hitting a string of green lights, the taxi continued to cruise without stopping once.

"Ah, it was Yuko!" Shuichi exclaimed to himself.

His wife was able to track his location using the GPS function on her smartphone.

After their conversation, Yuko must have arranged for a taxi to pick him up from his location under the name "Okada," then set the destination for Miyabi Junior High School. If that were the case, when he flagged down the taxi, the driver could have asked, "Are you Okada-san?" At any rate, that was the only explanation that made sense.

"Did my wife call you?"

"Well, no, I saw you raising your hand."

"Then how do you know my name? Where I'm

going, the name of my kid's school—how do you know all that?"

"How? Some things are difficult to explain . . ." The driver made a weary face and scratched his head. "I don't blame you for being shocked. When you know, you know . . . is about all I can say."

"That's not good enough," Shuichi spat out in irritation.

"I didn't think so." The driver grimaced as the taxi sped on its way.

"Anyway, as your driver, my job isn't to convince you how I know where you want to go but to deliver you safely to your destination, so it doesn't matter whether I've convinced you or not. Besides, not everything in this world can be explained. That's just how some things work."

Since the driver didn't appear to be anyone suspicious, Shuichi considered sitting there quietly, but the more he thought about the situation, the more unsettling it became.

Then, the fare meter caught his eye.

It read 69,820.

Suddenly, Shuichi shot up from his seat and leaned forward, grabbing hold of the back of the passenger seat.

"Hey! You *are* a scam artist after all! Pretending like you're some kind of detective, digging into people's lives, then charging them this ridiculous amount."

The moment Shuichi raised his voice, the meter ticked to 69,730.

"Huh? What was that?!"

"We're going to get into an accident if you keep yelling in my ear. Please sit down. We've been strictly instructed to make sure that passengers wear their seat belts, so buckle up, please."

"Never mind that. Why is the fare so ridiculously high? Plus, the number on the meter went down. What's the matter with the meter? It's broken."

The driver flitted a glance at the meter and smiled. "Oh, this? It's not broken."

"What? What's going on with this taxi? You know what? Forget it. Just let me off."

The driver let out a sigh. "I guess you leave me no

choice. Okay, I'll explain, but will you calm down first? Put on your seat belt, please. It's all right. I promise to let you off when we arrive at Miyabi."

"You don't expect me to pay—"

"It's all right," the driver repeated firmly.

Shuichi crossly leaned back in the seat and folded his arms.

He glared at the driver's reflection as if to say "This better be good."

The driver met his gaze but made no sign of talking.

Relenting, Shuichi moved to buckle his seat belt, and at the sound of the click, the driver's face brightened. "Thank you."

It was either thanks for wearing a seat belt or thanks for being willing to listen, one of the two.

"I'm going to take us the long way a bit."

"What?"

"Not the road. My explanation."

"Whatever. Just start talking," Shuichi said, keeping his arms knotted across his chest. The meter ticked: 69,640. The fare was definitely decreasing.

"Hmm, where to start."

The driver, looking thoughtful for a moment, made a left turn. When he came out of the turn, he asked, "Do you consider yourself lucky, Okada-san?"

"Lucky? Why are you asking?"

"Humor me, please. Would you consider yourself the lucky type? Or . . ."

"Hmph, life hardly ever gives you good things. I couldn't tell you anything about a lucky life. My life's been nothing but a series of unfortunate events."

"I see. Well, my job is to change the fortunes of someone like that."

"What in the heck kind of job is that?"

"Like I said, I'm your driver. That's what I've been trying to tell you from the start. I'm *your* driver."

This confused Shuichi even more.

"So, you're telling me your job is to change my luck? Now I really don't get it. You're a driver. Isn't it your job to take passengers to where they want to go?"

"No, my job is turning people's luck around. I'm not driving you to where you want to go, Okada-san. I'm driving you somewhere you'll encounter a turning point in your life."

"That sounds like you're sticking your nose where it doesn't belong. Taking me somewhere that you think will change my luck instead of where I want to go."

"It's still my job, regardless. You may not understand it now, but you will eventually. There's Miyabi Junior High."

"What?"

Shuichi looked out the window. They were driving through a neighborhood that seemed familiar.

It should have taken forty minutes by car to get from where Shuichi had been picked up to Yumeka's school. Had that much time passed already?

The driver pulled up in front of the main gate, and the automatic rear door popped open.

"You made it in time." The driver turned around and smiled at him.

The meter read 69,370.

"You know I'm not paying that ridiculous fare," Shuichi said, pointing to the meter.

The driver smiled again and said, "Of course not. You're free to ride as much as you'd like until the meter hits zero."

The tense expression on Shuichi's face softened. "What? You don't want me to pay?"

The driver nodded emphatically. "You should hurry. Otherwise, we would have sped all this way for nothing."

Shuichi glanced at his watch. It was five minutes before the start of the meeting. That meant that it had only taken ten minutes to get here.

"O-okay . . ."

Even after getting out of the car, Shuichi dwelled on whether he really didn't need to pay, but the rear door swung shut automatically. The taxi took off and soon disappeared around the corner.

Puzzled by the strange occurrence that just took place, Shuichi headed for the classroom.

"What was with that guy?"

YUMEKA STOPPED GOING TO SCHOOL DURING THE second year of junior high school. She was experiencing what was commonly known as "school refusal." She used to cheerfully say "I'm going now!" before heading off to elementary school, but that all changed when she entered junior high school. Though she didn't exactly enjoy school, she still managed to attend through the first year, but upon entering the second year, she increasingly started taking days off, complaining of headaches.

Shuichi tried to find out if she'd fallen out with her friends or was being bullied, but neither seemed to be the case. It seemed that she simply didn't want to go.

Perhaps he was being rigid in thinking that wasn't a valid reason to miss school, but apparently, there were other kids like her in class. Shuichi thought skipping school and missing out on seeing friends would be boring, but surprisingly, that wasn't necessarily the case. With a smartphone, they could stay connected with everyone without having to attend school.

Since both Shuichi and Yuko worked, they were out of the house all day, so they had no idea what Yumeka was doing on the days she missed school. She seemed to spend day and night at home messing around on her smartphone. At least, that was the impression that Shuichi got when he came home from work. Then, when morning came, she would complain, "I have a headache."

One time, Shuichi told her, "I know you have a headache, but considering your future, maybe you ought to try toughing it out."

"You say that because you don't know how much my head hurts," countered Yumeka. She then turned away, clutching her smartphone, and shut herself in her room. Despite his attempts to get her to open up, Shuichi had to go to work, leaving them with no opportunity to talk. Since Yuko held a leadership role at her part-time job, she couldn't easily take time off either, making it difficult for her to check in on their daughter. Thus, despite their desire for Yumeka to go to school, they found themselves powerless to do anything about it.

When Yuko warned, "If you keep goofing off on your phone, I'll take it away," Yumeka shot back, "I haven't even touched it." They considered installing cameras in the house to monitor her behavior but, ultimately, decided against it because it would violate her trust.

Despite their best efforts to push her to go to school, Yumeka's refusal continued to grow and solidify with every passing day.

Perhaps it all boiled down to Yumeka being at a difficult age.

ALTHOUGH YUMEKA'S HOMEROOM TEACHER, HIGAshide, was the one to suggest a meeting, he didn't seem to have anything specific to discuss. He merely asked about Yumeka's behavior at home, encouraged her to try to come to school if she was feeling up to it, and otherwise offered platitudes that hardly qualified as advice.

He wore a smile throughout. He seemed to be the cheerful sort and, according to Yumeka, had a young daughter, so he was probably in his late twenties or early thirties. Although he didn't give off a bad impression, the superficiality of the conversation left Shuichi feeling that the meeting was merely to document Higashide had done what he could as a teacher in case a problem arose later. This dampened Shuichi's desire to have a serious discussion about Yumeka.

In the first place, why had he been called out of work to have a conversation that could have easily taken place on the phone?

Even as they were discussing the serious issue of school refusal, the fact that Higashide asked about Yumeka's well-being with a smile on his face, as if to imply that he bore no responsibility in this, angered Shuichi.

Shuichi had no intention of blaming the teacher, of course, but he found it strange that Yumeka's homeroom teacher wouldn't feel the slightest responsibility. Shuichi refrained from saying anything because he didn't want to come across as vindictive.

Still, as the conversation continued and Shuichi began to wish for a more substantive discussion, his frustration became increasingly stamped on his face.

Sensing this, Yuko became more talkative and steered the conversation toward noncontroversial topics, until eventually, Higashide concluded, "We'll continue to monitor the situation and take it from there," ending the meeting exactly thirty minutes after it began.

Everything wrapped up according to schedule.

Finding it absurd to end the meeting with a smile, Shuichi got up from his chair and headed immediately for the door, until he heard Higashide's voice at his back:

"I'm sorry to have interrupted your workday."

Without acknowledging the apology, Shuichi stopped just long enough to say a terse "thank you" and left the classroom.

After Yuko bowed apologetically to Higashide, she went out and caught up with Shuichi.

"What's going on with you?" she asked Shuichi, whose mood had clearly soured during the meeting.

He stalked down the hall, saying nothing.

"What's got you in a bad mood suddenly?"

He stopped to address Yuko's probing questions. "I

don't have time for pointless discussions. I got called out of work and took a taxi to be here only to find we could've easily had this conversation over the phone."

"Maybe, but the teacher made time for us because he wanted to help."

"That wasn't how it looked to me. Besides, I don't have time for this." Shuichi raised his voice.

The insurance premiums for twenty lost clients were about to be deducted from his next paycheck. Not only that, he was required to refund the premiums for the ten months paid so far. It was also doubtful he would receive a bonus. He needed to secure as many contracts as possible before the next payday to minimize the damage. He didn't have any time to waste by being here. Yuko, unaware of the situation, was understandably left speechless by his irritable mood.

"Anyway, I have to go back to the office."

With this, Shuichi turned his back and hurried off.

He knew that it would be better to explain the situation to Yuko, but what if he was able to secure some miraculous contracts to recover his losses? Considering this, he believed that it wouldn't be too late to tell Yuko once the next paycheck was finalized.

No, thinking about it calmly, he recognized the game was already over. That was why he needed to be honest with Yuko and tell her not only about the trip but also about their future.

But Shuichi didn't have the courage. He was no different from a child avoiding his problems, hoping they would disappear on their own.

As he cut across the schoolyard alone, he tried desperately to figure out what to do. But no amount of thinking was going to lead him to a solution. He was at an impasse. Still, he had no choice but to keep trying.

Try?

He didn't know what the word meant anymore.

He had stormed out of the meeting, saying, "I'm too busy. I don't have time for this," but then what? What was he supposed to do? Where was he supposed to go, and what should he focus on, and how?

Shuichi had lost sight of the answers.

REWARDS CARD

Wakiya kept quiet throughout the morning meeting.

Shuichi had greeted him upon arriving at the office, but Wakiya had only returned a muted "Morning."

His face was vacant as if he was trying to figure out what to say to Shuichi.

Unable to bear the awkwardness, Shuichi left the office as soon as the meeting ended.

Part of him hoped that his leaving would give the impression that he was trying everything he could to recover as many contracts as possible.

"I'm going out for a bit," he announced, casting a glance at Wakiya.

Amidst the usual chorus of "See you later," Wakiya continued to page through the documents on his desk without looking in Shuichi's direction. Shuichi hurried out of the office and pondered his next move as the elevator descended. When he exited the building, he still didn't have an answer. Though it was barely past nine, the heat radiating from the asphalt almost made him black out. The day was already shaping up to be another scorcher.

As he started to walk toward the train station, he spotted a taxi approaching.

No, it can't be.

The taxi pulled up next to him and popped open the rear door even though he hadn't signaled for it. Shuichi looked at the driver's face through the window. It was the driver from yesterday. If Shuichi recalled correctly, the man's name was Takushi Omakase.

Shuichi hesitated for a moment. With everything that had happened since the day before, he had forgotten about the taxi. Thinking about it now, he found it all quite strange. Seeing the same taxi pull up in front of him again, he couldn't help but think the driver was following him.

Peering into the open door, Shuichi grumbled, "You're here to collect on yesterday's ride, aren't you?"

"I wouldn't dream of it! Like I said yesterday, you're free to ride as much as you'd like until the meter hits zero. Come on, hop in."

Shuichi looked at the meter.

69,370.

It hadn't moved since he got out the day before, not that he'd made a point of keeping track.

"Hop in? Do you even know where I'm headed?"

It was a mean-spirited question. The day before, the driver had started driving toward Yumeka's school unprompted, claiming his years of experience would tell him where someone needed to go. That day, not even Shuichi himself knew where he wanted to go. And yet the taxi had stopped for him again. Just where was it going to take him this time?

The driver replied immediately, "I'll take you to where you need to go, just like yesterday."

The driver's words stirred an irresistible urge within Shuichi. Truth be told, he had run out of the office without a destination in mind. He climbed into the back seat.

"Watch your fingers."

No sooner had the driver spoken than the rear door swung shut and the taxi glided onto the road. Shuichi fixed his gaze on the driver's face in the rearview mirror. He seemed relaxed, showing no sign of tension.

"How did you know where to find me?" Shuichi asked suspiciously.

"As I told you before, I've been at this for a very long time. It's my job to know. You're looking at a pro." He chuckled.

Shuichi didn't find the answer very helpful, but it

seemed he wasn't going to get a satisfactory answer no matter what he asked. He heaved a sigh.

"Hey, wait a minute," said the driver upon seeing Shuichi's reaction.

"What?" Shuichi said crossly.

"Have you not noticed a change in luck since we met yesterday?"

"Huh?" Shuichi tried to recall what the driver had told him before.

My job is turning people's luck around. I'm not driving you to where you want to go, Okada-san. I'm driving you somewhere you'll encounter a turning point in your life.

Yes, that was it. Shuichi snickered at the recollection.

"Change in luck? All you did was waste time I didn't have. Sure, I made it to the meeting on time, but it turned out to be completely pointless. We could have had the conversation over the phone instead of pulling me away from work just to piss me—"

"Gah! I knew it!" the driver exclaimed, slapping

the steering wheel. "I had a sneaking suspicion that was going to happen."

"What are you talking about?"

"Now, don't get upset."

Noticing the young man smirking, Shuichi snapped, "You don't know anything about me!"

The driver continued, undeterred, "But I do. You had twenty contracts, which were supporting your livelihood, canceled. This will not only slash your salary for the upcoming month but also require either refunding the ten months' worth of insurance premiums already paid or having that amount deducted from your salary and bonuses. Meanwhile, your daughter, who is going through a rebellious stage, refuses to go to school and won't listen to you; on top of which, your wife, unaware of the financial situation, has got her head filled with the Paris trip. And if that wasn't enough, you received a troubling call from your mother, so you were in no mood to get called into school to have a meaningless conversation."

Shuichi was struck speechless.

THE LUCKY RIDE

He wanted to ask how in the world the driver knew all that but was too shocked to form the words.

"Look, Okada-san. I understand why you would lose patience under those circumstances. I told you my job is to take you somewhere your luck would change for the better, and from there, your fortune was going to be dramatically transformed. Well, it was *supposed* to, but you let that chance slip away."

"H-how do you mean?" Shuichi asked, bewildered.

"Do you know what your wife and the homeroom teacher, Higashide-san, were talking about before you arrived?"

"They weren't talking about Yumeka?"

The driver shook his head. "They were talking about your job."

"My job?"

"That's right. The subject of your job came up when your wife told him you couldn't attend the meeting. When she mentioned that you sell insurance, he expressed an interest in hearing more. From there, not only would Higashide-san reconsider his insurance options, but many of the other teachers at the school as well. Several years later, as those teachers moved on to other schools, it also would have led to more contracts for you. That's what was supposed to happen."

"H-hold on a minute." Shuichi stopped the conversation to collect his thoughts. "How do you know that?"

"As I said before, there are some things I just can't explain. Some things you know from experience. Like catching a flyball in the outfield, for example. How do you know where a ball is going to fall? Determining that isn't a matter of calculation but experience, right? You take into account the ball's velocity and spin rate, the direction of the wind and the ball's launch angle, the sound of the bat hitting the ball, and where on the bat the ball made contact. Pitch velocity and the batter's muscle mass. There are so many variables that go into determining where the ball will drop, and they're all intertwined. If you try to calculate the landing point after considering all those variables, it's much too complicated to come up with the correct answer no matter how much time you have. But with experience, you just know. It's like that."

The driver glanced at Shuichi through the mirror and frowned. Perhaps it was the wrong choice of analogy, as Shuichi showed no sign of understanding.

"At any rate, this is the important part, so please keep it in mind," the driver continued. "There are moments in life when your luck can dramatically change, and places like that exist for everyone. Everyone has a sensor capable of picking up on it. The sensor is most sensitive when you're in a good mood. Conversely, it doesn't work when you're in a bad mood. So, even when you're in the presence of a lucky opportunity, if you're in a bad mood and your sensor isn't working, you'll miss out on that luck. Just like what happened to you yesterday."

"If you're in a bad mood, you miss out on luck?"

"That's right. A bad-tempered person can be in the luckiest of places and not even notice it. They're irritated, thinking only of leaving as quickly as possible. That's why you need to maintain a good mood. Now, my job is to take you to the place where your luck will turn for the better, so the idea of you being in a bad mood at the place I've taken you to is, well . . . it's just unthinkable. Please make sure that doesn't happen next time."

"Being in a bad mood is unthinkable . . ."

"I'll say it again. If you don't maintain a good mood, you won't be able to sense your luck turning. A bad-tempered person might unknowingly wish for life-changing opportunities to go away."

"Hold on," Shuichi interrupted again. "You mean to tell me that if I had been in a good mood with Yumeka's teacher yesterday, my luck would have changed, leading me to land a bunch of contracts?"

"That's right. Even by a conservative estimate, you could have secured fifty new contracts over the next two years. You would have been well on your way to setting a sales record at your company and becoming a top salesman."

"Did you say fifty new contracts in two years?"

Shuichi scoffed. "You expect me to believe in such a dramatic turnaround?"

The driver sighed and shook his head. "It's all right if you don't. Whether you believe me or not is entirely up to you."

The driver fell silent and focused on the road for a while.

Slowly, Shuichi began to understand that the driver was telling him the truth. He simply knew too much about Shuichi. If he had such an accurate grasp of Shuichi's current situation, it wouldn't be all that strange if he knew something about his future too. In which case, the driver was telling the truth. Shuichi had missed a golden opportunity to secure a haul of contracts, starting with Yumeka's teacher, all because he had been in a bad mood.

"I don't know what's going on, but what you're telling me is the truth, is that it?" he asked, his voice still tinged with doubt.

"Listen, Okada-san. I'm here as your driver. My job is to turn your luck around, and it doesn't do me any good to lie. Besides . . ."

"Besides what?"

"Even if my vision of the future is all in my head, do you think an irritable insurance salesman stands a chance at landing a new contract?"

"I, uh . . ."

Shuichi fell silent.

WHEN SHUICHI HAD FIRST CHANGED CAREERS AND joined his current company, he had been worried about whether he could succeed in the job. Shuichi instantly realized from observing Wakiya up close that his boss was an exceptional salesman. Even though Wakiya didn't go out on sales calls, new contracts always seemed to come to him. Clients sought him out naturally, no matter what he did. That was the kind of salesman Wakiya was. One night at an izakaya, Shuichi had asked him what was the secret behind his success.

Wakiya said in response, "Always be cheerful and happy. No matter when, no matter what."

"Is that it?" Shuichi asked, feeling somewhat let down by the answer.

"That's it. Insurance is something everyone needs in life, so anyone can potentially become a client. But no one conveniently signs up when you want them to. The key is to be the person who comes to mind when they're ready to sign. So, be cheerful and happy, no matter when, no matter what."

"Okay . . ."

Wakiya grinned. "You look like you were expecting to hear something more profound. Eh, that's okay. But you know, the 'no matter when, no matter what' part isn't as easy as it sounds."

With that, Shuichi had watched Wakiya take a pull from his beer.

"You're right," Shuichi now admitted to the driver. "I wouldn't want to purchase insurance from someone in a bad mood. I've likely missed my fair share of chances because of it. Now look at me."

Seeming worried that he might have been too harsh, the driver hastily said in a cheerful tone, "Well,

I understand the feeling. It's not just insurance. No one who's in a perpetually bad mood is going to be successful in any profession. On the other hand, all you need is to maintain a good mood to recognize when your is luck turning. It's a missed opportunity. What's important is that you do so from now on. So, make sure you're in a good mood next time."

"Next time?"

This guy is going to keep showing up before me, he thought, recalling what the driver had told him yesterday.

"So, you're going to keep showing up until the meter hits zero, is that it?"

"That's right."

"And I get to ride for free?"

"You can."

"But why . . . are you giving me rides worth tens of thousands of yen for free to take me to places where my luck is supposed to improve?"

The driver glanced at him through the mirror.

"Why? Because it's my job. I don't blame you for

being suspicious, but I promise I won't charge you a thing. You have my word, so relax. The bill has already been paid in full."

"Huh?"

Did he mean to say someone other than Shuichi had paid the exorbitant amount in advance? If so, who was it?

Just as Shuichi began to raise the question, the driver interjected, "By the way—"

Shuichi held back his words.

"It's not yen," the driver said.

"What now?"

"It's points."

"Points?"

"That's right. You have 69,280 points to ride for free."

Although Shuichi couldn't be sure, it seemed the driver was telling him that the number on the meter represented points rather than yen. If that was the case, what was even more confusing was what the points were awarded for.

Shuichi cracked a wry smile and said, "I've been listening to you since yesterday, but I can't make heads or tails of what you're going on about. It is part of your job as a professional driver to ensure the passenger has a pleasant ride, isn't it?"

The driver nodded. "You're right."

Reaching across to the passenger side, the driver opened the glove compartment and took something out. Holding it out toward Shuichi sitting in the back, he continued to drive with his other hand, his eyes focused on the road.

Shuichi reached out and took the item with some trepidation.

"What's this?"

It was a folded piece of paper the size of a business card. He had a vague memory of having seen it before but couldn't quite place where. The illustration printed on it looked oddly familiar. The style of the artwork appeared to be from another era and the cardstock yellowed with age. Perhaps it was a membership card or a rewards card for some store. He unfolded it and finally understood what it was.

Novelty Shop Okada.

The rewards card, on which the address and phone number of his family home were printed, was filled with thirty stamps in the designated squares. It had a value of five hundred yen, but it didn't appear to have been redeemed.

"Where did you get this?"

"From the shop, of course."

"Knock it off. This is the rewards card for my family's shop that closed years ago. How do you have it?"

"As a professional whose job it is to change someone's fortunes, please allow me to explain something about luck."

Instead of answering Shuichi's question, the driver began a different story.

"Do you remember the question I asked you yesterday?"

"What question?"

"I asked if you considered yourself lucky."

"Sure, I remember," replied Shuichi despondently.

"Well, I was lying to you then."

"Lying?"

"I told you that my job was to drive you somewhere your luck would improve because I thought you might find that easier to understand. But the truth is there's no such thing as good or bad luck."

"Say that again."

"There's no such thing as lucky people or unlucky people. That's not how luck works."

"You can't be serious. Nothing is going right for me these days, while good things keep happening to the lucky ones."

The driver let out a polite laugh. "You don't really believe that, do you?"

Shuichi drew his brows into a knot, bristling at the driver's attitude.

"Do you think the lucky ones, as you called them, keep on getting lucky without expending any effort?"

"Wha—" For a moment, Shuichi froze before answering, "Well, no. I'm saying that some people always have good things happen to them, while others don't, despite putting in the same amount of effort."

"So, you're saying that you put in just as much effort as the lucky ones but don't experience the same positive outcomes?"

"I wasn't necessarily talking about myself. I meant that's what happens generally."

"No, it doesn't," said the driver bluntly. "Listen, Okada-san. Luck works like a post-payment. Good things don't happen without you taking a corresponding action. Can you get something without saving up first? No one in their right mind would expect that. But when it comes to luck, it's the people who don't do anything to save points that expect it most."

Shuichi stared at the rewards card in his hand.

"That card has a value of five hundred yen," the driver explained. "Do you know why? That's because there are points saved up on it. Have you ever received a card that lets you spend five hundred yen first before saving anything up? No such card exists. It's the same with luck. Yet when people talk about 'being lucky,' they expect something good to happen suddenly, ignoring the effort that took place beforehand."

"Are you telling me that luck works the same way as this rewards card?"

"Yup. Luck isn't something that should be described as good or bad. It's more like something you save and spend. First, you save it up, and once you've accumulated a decent amount, you spend it. Some people like to use it as soon as they've saved up a bit, while others prefer to save big, then spend big. It's different for every person. At any rate, those people considered to be lucky are merely using the luck they've saved."

As Shuichi continued to stare at the rewards card, he echoed the driver's words. "Luck isn't good or bad but something you save and spend . . ."

"You can't blame the store for not allowing you to use points if you haven't saved any, right? It's the same with luck. Many people complain about not being able to spend any luck or wonder 'Why always him?' without saving up any themselves."

"So, the lucky ones appear to work as hard as the unlucky ones, but in reality, they've just been accumulating luck?"

"Right. When someone uses the luck that they've accumulated, it appears to others that they're lucky."

As Shuichi folded his arms across his chest, his expression was grim.

"No, that can't be," he said, shaking his head. "There have to be lucky people, just as there are unlucky ones. Some people grow up to have a comfortable life without any hardships, while others are struck by misfortune after misfortune no matter how hard they try. It's the same in competition. A victory isn't guaranteed just because you put in the effort. Some people work harder than anyone and still end up losing. What you're talking about sounds nice, but reality isn't so kind. That's just your youthful idealism talking . . ."

The driver shot a glance at Shuichi through the mirror.

Their eyes met, but Shuichi continued, "You'll understand someday when you're my age."

The driver grinned. "I don't see how age has anything to do with it. In any case, when you work hard and don't see any results, it means you're accumulating luck. The ones that see immediate results or have something positive happen to them are simply using their accumulated luck a little at a time. It doesn't necessarily mean they're luckier than others. The ones who put in the same amount of effort but don't see immediate success are saving up luck that will pay off later in a much bigger way."

With that, the driver pulled over to the side of the road and popped open the rear door. "I wish we could continue our conversation, but we're here."

Shuichi looked out the window. The neighborhood wasn't one he recognized.

"Where are we?"

"Where you need to be right now," the driver declared.

Shuichi checked the fare meter. It read 62,130. The ride felt about as long as the last time, but the meter seemed to have decreased more rapidly. Since the ride was free, however, he didn't have anything to complain about.

As Shuichi got out of the car, the driver said, "Don't

forget, Okada-san. Think happy thoughts. If you're in a bad mood, your sensor won't be as sensitive to an opportunity," and shut the rear door. The taxi took off immediately.

"Tsk . . . mind your own business," Shuichi mumbled almost inaudibly at the taxi speeding away.

WHEN THE TAXI WAS OUT OF SIGHT, SHUICHI TOOK a moment to size up the building before him. The modest arcade, appearing to date back to the mid-Showa Era, was named the Gingko Shopping Street. He stood at the edge of the row, facing a store called the Gingko Café.

This is the place that will turn my luck around?

The building seemed old, but the café itself appeared to be quite new.

The blue wooden door against the white wall was eye-catching. The neatly arranged windows provided a clear view into the shop. Two pairs of customers were seated at some small tables in the rear, and another was at the enormous communal table in the middle of the café. The interior emanated a welcoming ambiance. While Shuichi didn't believe everything the driver had said, he recognized that the man possessed a peculiar ability. Though he couldn't admit as much to the driver directly, he now reached for the blue door, tingling with anticipation.

Good mood, positive thoughts, he reminded himself.

As soon as he opened the door, he caught the eye of the man sitting alone at the enormous table on the right. Shuichi casually put on a smile and acknowledged him with a nod. The man smiled and nodded back. The table was large enough to accommodate ten customers, but the man was the only one seated. Judging from the way the man chatted with the female staff worker who brought him his coffee, Shuichi pegged him for a regular. The two pairs of women at the tables in the rear appeared to be mom friends. He decided to sit near the man at the center table, but rather than take the seat directly across, which would have seemed odd, he moved one seat to the left, so they were seated diagonally across from one another. The man appeared to be around thirty. With the chiffon cake and the coffee he'd ordered set aside, he focused on the laptop before him. The tapping of the keys echoed pleasantly.

Could this be the man who'll change my fate?

It could be someone who had yet to walk through the door, or perhaps it was the female staff worker chatting with the man now. If what the driver said was true, then either someone in the café or someone who would arrive later held the key to turning his fortune around.

"Welcome."

Another woman greeted Shuichi, setting a water and a menu on the table.

"I'd like a coffee," said Shuichi in a cheerful tone, putting on his best smile.

"One coffee. Will that be all?" The woman beamed back.

"Yes, please."

Shuichi wasn't exactly sure what he was supposed

to do, but he did his best to stay positive. Maintaining a casual smile, he took a moment to take in his surroundings.

Although the café looked new, the walls and floor appeared to be made from reclaimed wood, giving it a rustic charm. The tables and chairs were likely handpicked with care. They appeared to be antique pieces rather than items made from reclaimed wood.

In such a small space, nuances such as the tone of conversation between customers and staff were conspicuous. Shuichi gathered that the woman who had brought him his water was likely the café's owner.

Before long, a cup of coffee was brought to his table. Shuichi had come to the café without knowing who or what he was waiting for, and as time passed without any clear sign of change, it seemed improbable that anything was going to happen. Shuichi decided to say something the next time he made eye contact with the man sitting across from him.

Sure enough, that moment arrived almost immediately. The determined gaze of someone sitting diagonally across from you couldn't be ignored for too long.

"Is that any good?"

Shuichi pointed to the chiffon cake in front of the man.

"Uh, yeah," answered the man with a hint of surprise, smiling politely. His hands stopped typing.

"I just might have to order one for myself."

"Sure, why not."

The man smiled again, appearing a bit unsure of how to respond, and directed his gaze back to his laptop.

"Excuse me, can I have a slice of what he's having?" Shuichi called out to one of the staff, nodding toward the cake.

"Sure thing," the woman replied and disappeared behind the counter.

"Gosh, it looks so good when it's right in front of you," Shuichi muttered to himself, stealing a look at the man's reaction. He was desperate to find some way to start a conversation. The man briefly pushed a smile across his lips, then went back to typing on his laptop. He seemed to not want to be bothered.

Maybe it isn't him.

Though the thought flashed across his mind, he did his best to maintain a cheerful attitude and waited for the chiffon cake to arrive.

The woman set down the cake in front of him and said, "Thanks for waiting," even though she'd brought it rather quickly.

"Thank you," he said with a smile. The woman smiled back.

Could it be her?

Shuichi scooped up a forkful of chiffon cake and tasted it.

"Wow, this is delicious!"

In the cozy space of the café, he didn't have to raise his voice to be heard. No doubt everyone in the café heard him.

Turning to the owner and staff behind the counter, Shuichi said, "This is very good," before turning to the young man across from him.

"I'm glad I ordered this. Thanks for the tip."

The women behind the counter smiled, but the man, his face contorted into a grimace, stayed focused on the laptop screen and continued to type.

Again, Shuichi called out to the women behind the counter, "As someone who frequently holds insurance sales meetings in cafés like this one, I've tasted quite a few cakes in my day, but this chiffon cake is the best I've ever had. I mean it."

He said it loudly enough so the two groups of moms at the small tables could hear.

"Thanks very much," the owner answered with a sincere smile, then quickly went back to washing the dishes.

There was no noticeable reaction from the moms in the back. The man continued to focus on the computer screen. No one seemed to react to Shuichi's mention of insurance sales.

What am I doing?

Shuichi inwardly clicked his tongue. The smiling face of the taxi driver flashed through his mind.

Falling for that driver's lies and putting on this friendly act. No one here is interested in insurance!

Just as Shuichi decided to leave the café as soon as he finished his cake, the door opened, and in walked a new customer.

Not this guy . . . ?

Shuichi watched in disbelief as the man, who appeared to be in his late forties, quickly found and approached the man sitting across from him, saying, "I'm sorry to keep you waiting, Sensei!"

"Let's go over there." The man in front of Shuichi stopped the newcomer from sitting down and led him toward the back, where they could talk more privately, leaving Shuichi alone at the enormous table.

At that moment, Shuichi's phone vibrated. The call was from Wakiya, but he chose not to answer it. Since the company-issued phone had GPS tracking, Wakiya would know exactly where he was.

He could say that he was occupied in a meeting at the café, but he couldn't stay much longer regardless. He was angry at himself for falling for the driver's story and desperately looking for an encounter that would change his luck.

He played me for a fool! I don't have that kind of time!

Shuichi got up and paid the bill at the counter. Receiving his change from the owner, he asked, "Excuse me, is there a train station nearby?"

The owner looked a bit surprised but then smiled and answered, "If you go left out the door and continue straight, you'll run into the station. You can't miss it."

Shuichi went outside and glanced back through the window of the café. No one seemed to notice his departure.

"Tsk, where the hell am I, anyway?"

He left the café, prickling with irritation.

SEEDS OF HAPPINESS

When Shuichi reached the train station, he discovered that he was at a place called Seya, about twenty minutes west of Yokohama Station by train. It would take him an hour and a half to return to the office.

Bringing me all the way out here, for God's sake.

Shuichi's anger toward the driver continued to swell inside him.

Though it was daytime, the scene outside the train

window suddenly grew dark. The sky, which was clear only moments ago, became shrouded in dense clouds, thunder rumbling in the distance. No sooner did he think, "Here it comes," than the rain began to streak down the window.

By the time he arrived at the station nearest his office, a torrential downpour pounded the pavement, the resulting spray turning the roads hazy with mist. Not a single pedestrian in sight. Due to poor visibility, cars crept along barely faster than walking speed.

A long line had already formed at the taxi stand in front of the station. People stood beneath a flimsy roof, soaked from the torso down, waiting for a taxi that might never come.

Eager to return to the office as quickly as possible, Shuichi bought a cheap umbrella at the convenience store inside the station and went outside. Within seconds, he was drenched from head to toe, rendering the umbrella useless. The only part of him that wasn't wet was from his neck up.

"Damn it!"

Although the office was only a five-minute walk

from the station, it was far enough to thoroughly soak him as if he'd taken a shower fully clothed.

"Now would be a good time to show up!" Shuichi exclaimed aloud.

It was a complaint directed at the driver. After all, it was the driver who had taken him to the outskirts of Yokohama, which was why it took him an hour and a half to return to the office, and if that wasn't enough, why he got caught in torrential rain.

"This is all his fault," he muttered aloud, but his voice was drowned out by the sound of the rain pelting the plastic umbrella.

Finally, when he ran into the building where his office was located, the rain had subsided somewhat, and by the time the elevator delivered him to the sixth floor and he looked out the window by the elevator hall, the rain appeared to have let up entirely.

"What in the hell was that?"

Shuichi headed directly for the office without any time to compose himself. He needed to see Wakiya right away.

"Hi, I'm back," said Shuichi wearily.

Seeing Shuichi panting for air as he entered the office, Wakiya let out a sigh as if he might bury his head in his hands at any moment.

"I was hoping to get a contract, but I struck out," reported Shuichi.

"I was going to send you to meet with one of my clients, but you can't go looking like that."

Wakiya had probably intended to introduce him to a client who was likely to renew their policy. But showing up to the meeting in a sweaty and rain-soaked suit would only give the client a bad impression.

"I'll go buy a new suit and change."

Wakiya shook his head. "There isn't enough time. I'll take the meeting myself."

Wakiya grabbed his bag, walked across the office, and moved his nameplate on the whiteboard to the column marked "Out for a meeting" as Shuichi watched in silence.

Unable to sit down in his wet clothes, Shuichi bypassed his desk, deciding to buy a towel at a convenience store nearby. As he stepped back out into the elevator hall, he noticed sunrays peeking out from the breaks in the clouds, illuminating the puddles that had formed on the ground outside.

Nothing is going right . . . Why is this happening to me?
Shuichi boarded the empty elevator and sighed.

There were times when everything seemed to go wrong. At these moments, he wondered whether he was cut out for the job. It wasn't that he wasn't working as hard as the others. In fact, he took his job more seriously than his colleagues. A few of them used "Out for a meeting" as an excuse to go out, watch a movie, hang out at a café—whatever they pleased. And yet their sales records were better than his. The aggravating reality was that despite his best efforts, everything seemed to backfire, while his colleagues, who slacked off, outperformed him. It was often said that results were everything. Nevertheless, he found it unbearable that he tried so hard only to end up looking like a fool.

Still, he persevered because he believed his efforts would be rewarded. But after having his contracts canceled en masse, being deceived by the odd driver, squandering an opportunity his boss set up for him to redeem himself, and to cap it all off, getting sopping wet in a torrential downpour as if to symbolize his bad luck, anyone would have taken these as signs to quit their job.

Shuichi pulled the newly purchased towel from its bag and, after tossing the bag in the trash, exited the convenience store.

Parked outside was the taxi with its rear door open.

Instantly, Shuichi felt a surge of anger rush to his head.

"You!"

Fearing that he might lose control if he gave in to his anger, he cautiously climbed into the back seat, clenching the towel to steady his trembling hands. "You better have a damn good explanation—"

"Okada-san, you're all wet!" the driver exclaimed before Shuichi could finish. "You can't sit in my taxi like that. Please put the towel on the seat before sitting down."

"Shut up!"

"Huh?" The driver blinked. "You look . . . mad?"

"Gee, do you think? Everything is a mess because of you!"

"What? Why? How can that be? You should be thanking me about now."

"I don't want to hear it. Look at me! Do I look like someone whose luck has turned for the better?"

The driver eyed him up and down. "No, I can't say that you do."

"Hmph, you sure know how to kick a man when he's down. Just whose fault do you think this is?"

"Well . . ."

The driver closed the rear door.

"It's mine."

"What?"

"It's my fault. It's my fault that your contracts got canceled, my fault that you can't secure any new ones, my fault that you lost your boss's trust, and my fault that you happened to get rained on. Let's see, anything else you want to blame me for? Ah, yes, it's my fault that you can't tell your wife about your disaster at work, my fault that your daughter refuses to go to school, and what else? Oh, yes, that your family business had to shut down."

Shuichi listened to the driver's rapid-fire recitation, dumbfounded. He struggled to mount a proper comeback.

Seeing this, the driver flashed a smirk. "There. Is that what you wanted to hear?"

"You . . ." Shuichi fought to find the words but came up empty. He simply wasn't the type to shout someone down into submission.

"Listen to me, Okada-san. You must never say the words, 'Whose fault do you think this is?' ever again. Frankly, it's because of you that things turned out this way."

"Because of *me*?"

"I told you to keep a good mood this morning, and just look at the mood you're in now. Can't you just admit that you're to blame for what happened?"

"I was in a good mood just like you told me. But that changed when I realized you deceived me. I tried keeping up my spirits, but nothing happened to turn my luck around."

"But that can't be. You were supposed to encounter a spectacular opportunity that few people would ever get."

"That's ridiculous. Nothing happened."

"You should have met a certain man there."

"I did, but he wasn't the least bit interested in insurance."

"Oh no." The driver momentarily looked up, then covered his face with his hands, groaning.

"What is it? What's wrong?"

"He wasn't interested in buying insurance. He was a celebrated writer."

"A writer?"

Shuichi recalled that the man in his late forties who'd come later had called the man "sensei." It had seemed strange that he was addressed as "sensei," because Shuichi had not guessed the man to be a doctor or a schoolteacher by the looks of him. But after hearing the driver's revelation, it now made sense.

"After meeting the writer, you were supposed to begin reading his books, which would go on to change your life. His books inspire you to quit your job and start something new. Consequently, your life takes off and—"

"Hold on. You said that a conversation with Yumeka's homeroom teacher would lead to me becoming a top salesman in the future. How did that future change to one where I'm quitting my job?"

"Well, of course, it changes. You had a chance at such a future then, but you let it slip away. That future isn't coming anymore. After all, life offers many different opportunities."

"How was I supposed to know that? I thought—"

"Okada-san, surely you took a moment to consider that securing a bunch of contracts isn't the only life-changing opportunity out there."

Based on the previous conversation with the driver, Shuichi had assumed that his life-changing opportunity would entail meeting someone who would drastically improve the number of insurance contracts he had, and hadn't taken a moment to consider anything else.

"How could anyone have known that?" Shuichi asked.

"It's difficult, I'll give you that. That's why I warned you. If you're not in the right mood, your sensor won't pick up the opportunity for change."

"But I was in a good mood," Shuichi insisted.

The driver shook his head as if to stop him from protesting. "No, I don't think you were, Okada-san. Are you sure you weren't just faking it? Just so you can get someone to purchase insurance?"

"You mean to tell me pretending's not going to cut it? How do you expect me to be cheerful when nothing good ever happens?"

"Ugh, we're still there, are we?" The driver expelled a deep sigh. "This conversation might take a while, so let's pause here for a moment. I was planning to take you to your next life-changing opportunity. But it seems you don't trust me. I'm happy to let you off here if you'd like. What will it be?"

Shuichi folded his arms across his chest and fell silent, looking hard into the driver's eyes. Eventually, he scowled and mumbled, "Let's go."

"I take it you want me to drive?" the driver asked to make doubly sure.

Shuichi gave him a reluctant nod.

"Okay, then. I'll get us on the road. We'll have some time before we reach our destination, so we should have a proper talk. So, this time, you won't miss your opportunity to turn your life around."

The driver turned on the blinker and prepared to pull the car out.

"Hold on a second. Wouldn't it be easier to just tell me the name of the writer I met earlier, instead of taking me to the next place?

"I can't do that."

"Why not?"

"Because I don't know."

"You don't know? As in you don't know who the writer is?"

"Right, I have no way of knowing that. I can only

see how the life-changing encounter will play out. Do you happen to remember his name, Okada-san?"

"No, I didn't ask."

The driver gave him an exaggerated shrug. "That's too bad. Anyway, we should get going."

Shuichi didn't answer but the taxi pulled away anyway. It seemed that once you let luck slip away, it was hard to get it back. With his arms still folded across his chest, Shuichi stared out the window and tried to sort out his thoughts.

OUTSIDE, THE SCENERY ROLLED PAST LIKE ANY OTHER taxi ride, yet they seemed to cover an impossible distance. It always seemed like they arrived at their destination in no time at all. Seeing Shuichi gazing outside the window, the driver began to speak.

"Do you see that man over there?"

Shuichi caught sight of an elderly man on the sidewalk. Apart from the leisurely way he was walking, nothing was notable about him.

"He's quite remarkable."

Shuichi didn't answer, but the driver continued.

"He's been an avid bonsai artist since he was young, and his arrangements have won quite a few awards, fetching prices of several million yen per pot. And see the short-haired woman on the opposite sidewalk coming toward us? The one holding hands with a child about elementary school age? She's famous too. Her dance school, which began with a few kids from the neighborhood, grew to become a much bigger school with many more students. Then, a kids' dance unit that got its start at the school went on to win numerous awards, and now she's set to become an instructor on a televised dance show."

"You could've fooled me." Shuichi grunted.

"Perhaps, but it's all true. Shall I stop the car? Would you like to talk to them?"

"Never mind that. I'm not interested in bonsai or dance. What are you getting at?"

"That amid our daily encounters, we come across people from all walks of life. We may not ever see them again, but each of them has led their own life. The seeds that produce miracles in our lives are all around us. Take the writer you met today, for example: If you fail to take an interest in getting to know him, he remains a stranger. You'll never know the life that he's led up to that point. Most people simply aren't interested in other's lives. No, they're infatuated with whether someone will become a client or make them richer in the wallet. But if you make an effort to genuinely connect with someone, they will cease to be a stranger and become an acquaintance, and over time, they may become a friend, or even a benefactor. Without knowing how to create these opportunities, luck will only pass you by, and you won't be able to grasp the seeds that produce miracles."

"And the key to creating these opportunities is being in a good mood."

"That's right. I mean, would you strike up a conversation with someone on the street who was in a foul mood? At a café? No, you'd only ask someone for directions or ask them to take a picture for you if they were in a good mood. It's the same at work. You wouldn't ask someone to do something for you if they looked upset, would you?"

"Then what's the problem with just pretending?"

"People aren't stupid, Okada-san. They're capable of seeing through the facade of an insurance salesman who is only thinking of securing a contract to improve their sales record."

"But that's how everyone operates. It isn't possible to be in a good mood every minute of the day."

"You're right. It isn't possible to maintain a good mood all the time. But don't you think that having 'negative' as your default attitude might be causing you to miss out on opportunities?"

"My default attitude isn't negative." Shuichi scoffed.

A smile floated to the driver's lips. Keeping one hand on the steering wheel, he took something out of the camera hanging above him next to the rearview mirror. Then with the other hand, he inserted it into the dashboard monitor.

"All of the taxis are equipped with these things lately. Were you aware?"

THE LUCKY RIDE

Onscreen, a video recording of the interior of the taxi began to play. It was a recording of Shuichi.

"Footage of you in the taxi," said the driver. "Many taxis record video inside the vehicle for security purposes."

It was a video of when Shuichi had first ridden in the taxi. He saw himself sitting in the back seat. There was no sound, but even to a biased observer, he didn't appear to be in a good mood.

It was the first time Shuichi was seeing himself on video. He was taken aback by how restless and fidgety he appeared. He was very different from the composed, reliable adult he had imagined himself to be, appearing more nervous, skittish. His embarrassment was such that he wished he could disappear into the ground.

"I'll turn up the sound."

The driver put his fingers on the dial and turned up the volume. The voice of the driver and a husky voice Shuichi didn't recognize soon filled the car.

There wasn't a moment of footage where his expression might be considered pleasant. After a while, the video switched to a recording of earlier that morning.

"I've seen enough," mumbled Shuichi, his face flushed in embarrassment. The driver stopped the video and removed the SD card, which he inserted back into the camera overhead.

"What do you say? Can you see the effort I'm making to engage you in conversation? Few people would bother being friendly to someone as miserable as you."

Shuichi couldn't deny that his expression was definitely crabby in the video. What's more, he was shocked to discover how different his appearance and voice were in the video compared to how he'd imagined them in his mind.

"I know what you're thinking: 'Who does he think he is, acting all high and mighty!' I understand that your work and family and your daughter are all crashing down on you at once. I understand the challenges you face. But all of that is merely a consequence of your negative attitude. Until you can correct that basic flaw, your life won't change, even if opportunities come your way. You're hardly alone in this, Okada-san. The world is filled with people whose default is negative, although they may not realize it themselves. You can see it on their faces on the commuter train. They're worried that they can't be happy. They're always lamenting, 'How can I be happy when only bad things happen.' But that isn't true. A person whose default is negative isn't capable of discovering the moments of happiness in daily life. That's all."

Shuichi gave up arguing. Though the driver was quite a bit younger than he was, his words rang true. Something in Shuichi's gut told him so. More than anything, he no longer cared to dispute the driver's assertions. At this moment, the desire to grasp on to anything that could change his current situation outweighed everything else.

He let out a deep sigh.

"Okay, I'll admit it. I had no idea my default attitude was negative, and you're right. Still, what can I do to be cheerful?"

"Perhaps you should get away from a profit-and-loss mindset."

"A profit-and-loss mindset?"

"Right. You tend to act when there's potential to profit and refrain when there's a possibility for loss. That mindset has become so ingrained in you that it's become second nature. Perhaps you should consider thinking in terms of 'fun' and 'interesting' when you're met with the unfamiliar."

"So you say, but what if I can't bring myself to feel that way?"

"Even though you may not find something interesting, remember that you're talking to someone who does. The least you can do is show interest and try to understand what they find enjoyable about it."

"And that would put me in a good mood?"

"A better mood than now."

"By doing . . . that?"

Despite Shuichi's skepticism, the driver smiled and continued, "By the way, there's something I forgot to mention."

"What is it?"

"Do you remember the elderly man and the short-haired woman on the sidewalk earlier?"

"Yeah, with the bonsai and the dance school."

"They both found fame through their hobbies. They also have the same job, and one more thing in common. Can you guess what it is?"

"I haven't a clue."

"They're in the insurance business."

"What?"

"And they're both members of the MDRT."

"The MDRT?!"

"I thought the name might ring a bell. It's an international organization of experts in life insurance and financial services. I've heard that you're required to secure quite a few contracts annually to earn membership."

"Wow, those two are way out of my league."

"Well, I don't know about that, but both have been clearing that benchmark for over a decade now. And did you notice? Amidst all the people walking by, those two were smiling. They were happy over nothing at all."

"Why didn't you tell me earlier?"

"You had your chance back there. Even if you've never tried bonsai or dance, simply thinking, 'That looks interesting,' or 'I wonder what's so enjoyable about it,' could have led you to strike up a conversation and become friends. After you're on friendly terms and come to learn that you're in the same line of business, they might have shared the secrets to their success. You say that you would have taken an interest if you'd known earlier, but it isn't possible to know everything from the start.

"So, you ought to reconsider that mindset of only acting when it's beneficial and refraining when it's not. You never know where or how things might connect. So, have I convinced you that it's better to find things interesting or enjoyable?"

"All right, I'll give it a try," Shuichi said, though the expression on his face was hesitant.

The driver smiled.

"Then I'd like to say one more thing while we're at it."

"Sure, let's have it," Shuichi responded, suddenly more open to listening to the driver's words.

"Do you remember when I said my job was to

take you somewhere your luck would turn for the better?"

"Yeah?"

"Do you know what's supposed to happen once you're there?"

"Huh? What's supposed to happen?"

Shuichi had assumed that the place where his luck would improve would be where he would secure a contract, but the earlier conversation suggested otherwise. It seemed that succeeding in the insurance business wasn't the only way to achieve his future happiness. In which case, there was no telling what would happen there.

After some hesitation, he finally admitted, "No, what is it? I'm not sure I follow."

"Nothing happens."

"What?" Shuichi furrowed his brows.

"There's that miserable look again."

As soon as the driver pointed this out, Shuichi hastily composed himself. He found it strange how attentively he was listening to the driver's words.

One reason for this was the driver's sudden and inexplicable appearance, a fact that could not be denied.

"Listen, improving your luck is, to put it another way, a turning point in life. It's a starting point from which your life gradually gets better, and not necessarily a place where something extraordinary happens. It's a place that you might look back on later and realize, 'This is where it all began.' So, it's not that nothing happens there, but that you might not feel like anything special happened."

"I won't feel anything?"

"Well, you should feel a slight change."

"A slight change, eh?" Shuichi repeated uncertainly.

"Okada-san, we discussed how, in life, there are many seeds of happiness scattered all around us."

"Seeds that are out of your grasp if you're in a bad mood."

"Yes, bad-tempered people spend their lives without so much as touching these seeds, but if you maintain a cheerful mood, you stand to collect many seeds."

"Yeah, I got that."

"Good, then this will be easy. Okada-san, have you ever grown vegetables from seeds?"

"Vegetables? No."

"Take carrots, for example. You plant the seeds in spring before the weather turns warm. When do you think they'll be ready to be harvested?"

"I don't know. In five months?"

"Oh, good. I was expecting you to say that same day."

"Hey, what do you take me for?"

"I'm joking, of course. But don't you think we have unrealistic expectations when it comes to the fruits of our labor?"

"Sure, we work hard so we want to see results right away."

"Yes, and we suffer because the results don't come fast enough. Some begin to wonder if they have bad luck. Those who believe their hard work is being overlooked have sown their seeds and are cultivating them and are merely crying over their carrots before they're ready to be harvested. In the long run, there's no such thing as effort going unrewarded. You're expecting too much for a brief period of effort, that's all. Expecting hard work today to yield results tomorrow simply isn't possible, even for the fastest-growing seeds."

Shuichi's face clouded. "But I don't have the time to wait. If I don't recover the contracts I lost before the next payday, I'm finished."

"You're not finished," countered the driver firmly. "Even if your income disappears and you lose your job, it's not the end. You simply start again from there. Everyone has the strength to do it. You don't have to worry."

Shuichi suddenly found himself tearing up as he looked at the driver. The driver's words held enough power to give Shuichi the courage to confront his troubles.

"Even me?"

"Even you. Even if the day comes when your worst-imagined scenario becomes a reality, as long as you have the courage to start from rock bottom, surely someday you will say the special words."

"Special words?"

"That's where it all began."

Perhaps overwhelmed by the unrelenting torrent of problems, Shuichi felt his eyes pool with tears. He sniffled hastily to keep them from falling.

"Okay." Shuichi chuckled in relief. "I feel better now."

"I'm glad to hear it." The driver scratched his head bashfully.

Watching the driver from behind, Shuichi tried to steady his breathing. For some reason he couldn't understand, Shuichi felt as if he did have the strength to start over simply because the driver told him so. The driver's words were the most supportive ones that Shuichi could possibly hear at that moment. Sniffling once more, Shuichi pushed up a smile. He no longer felt the need to wear an unhappy look.

"By the way, you mentioned just now that no effort goes unrewarded."

"Yes."

"You said that before too."

"Why, yes, I did."

"To this point, most of what you said has been spot-on, and I've been encouraged by your words, but when you mentioned that no effort goes unrewarded . . . I couldn't help but wonder if you weren't just saying that to lift my spirits."

"I wouldn't lie about something like that just to inspire you. It's the truth. No effort goes unrecognized." The driver glanced through the rearview mirror at Shuichi's face. "Hey? You don't seem too convinced. But perhaps we should save that conversation for another time. We've come to our destination."

The driver brought the car to a halt and opened the rear door.

Shuichi looked out the window to find it was dark out. He didn't recognize the location, but it was a bustling downtown area.

"Where are we?"

The driver smiled. "The place that will turn your luck around."

Shuichi got out of the car with a smile on his lips. Somehow, his rain-soaked suit had dried.

"Now, don't forget—"

"Stay cheerful. I got it."

"And?"

"No thinking in terms of profit and losses. Take an interest."

The driver gave Shuichi a nod, closed the door, then drove off.

TAXI

Shuichi looked at his surroundings. Though he didn't recognize the neighborhood, it was immediately apparent that he was in a busy part of town. Signs for hostess lounges and bars lined the cluster of mixed-tenant buildings. Many people were walking about, and taxis were coming and going on the streets. The ground floor of the building facing him was a bar.

"I guess this is it."

He looked up at the building as he made to step inside. The gray building with the narrow entryway was stacked with drinking establishments up to the top floor. Shuichi caught a glimpse of one of the signs on the side of the building and stopped in his tracks. There was a store with the name TAXI.

Shuichi let slip a smile. It seemed his life was fated to be changed by a taxi.

"This must be the place."

Turning around, he made his way to the elevator hall. He boarded the cramped elevator and pressed the old-fashioned button marked 5.

During the ride up, he repeated to himself, "Positive thoughts, stay cheerful."

Upon exiting the elevator, he found the entrance to the bar on the right. Though it wasn't apparent from the street, the ambiance emanating from the door was inviting. He went in and immediately noticed a tall bartender behind the counter on the right, who greeted him with a welcoming smile and a calm "Welcome in."

There was only one other customer sitting at the

far end of the counter, writing something in his notebook. The guitar case propped against the far wall appeared to belong to him. Shuichi sat at the counter, leaving three seats between them.

"What would you like?" asked the bartender.

"I'll have a beer to start."

Taking out his smartphone, Shuichi checked his location on Maps. The blue dot showed him inside the mixed-tenant building. He then zoomed out on the map and was dumbfounded.

"M-Matsuyama?!"

He quickly powered down the company-issued phone. Although it was after business hours, he didn't know what he'd say should his boss happen to check his location and ask what he was doing over nine hours away in Shikoku. The one consolation was that it was a Friday. Since he didn't have work the next day, he could make up any old excuse. Even if it hadn't been a Friday, he wouldn't have made it into the office the following morning anyhow.

Nevertheless, turning off the phone gave him some relief. That he was in Matsuyama was a fact that couldn't be changed, and this seemed like the place where his luck might finally turn. In which case, maintaining his cheerful mood and enjoying his current situation was the best thing he could do at the moment. Remarkably, he found himself able to reach that conclusion naturally.

I'm just going to enjoy whatever happens.

Once that decision was made, he felt himself in good spirits.

I get it. Being in a good mood isn't about expecting something interesting to happen but deciding to enjoy whatever happens.

Come to think of it, he had never allowed himself to enjoy a drink alone at a bar before. During his days at the car dealership and even at his current job, a typical night out involved carousing with his colleagues, so he couldn't help but feel uncertain about how to spend time alone at a bar like this. Yet a part of him didn't find it all that bad. A place where he could be alone without anyone bothering him and surrender himself to the music.

"Nice place you have here," Shuichi said to the bartender behind the counter, the words coming out of him effortlessly.

The bartender smiled and bowed his head.

Shuichi looked around the bar.

He caught the eye of the young man sitting at the left end of the counter. Shuichi flashed a smile, and the man responded in kind. Having closed the notebook he'd been writing in earlier, the man now sipped from a glass with a large chunk of ice. At first glance, he appeared quite young, but he might have been in his thirties.

"Do you come to this bar often?" Shuichi asked.

"Yes, well, on days that I have earned a bit, anyway. I'm rather fond of the atmosphere and the time I spend here. You could say that I work to be able to spend time here."

He seemed to say the last part jokingly.

"Do you play as a hobby?" Shuichi asked, casting a glance at the guitar case.

"It's actually how I make a living."

"Excuse me. I didn't realize you're a professional musician."

"Oh, nothing as respectable as that. I simply open my guitar case on the street and busk for tips. You might call that a professional musician, but most people would say that I'm a self-proclaimed musician. Or unemployed." The man chuckled lightheartedly.

"Then, you don't have . . ."

"Another job? No. I decided that I was going to live off my music—writing my songs and playing my guitar. My only indulgence is coming here to have a drink if I've had a good day . . . something like that."

"Wow, you're chasing your dream to become a star someday."

"I don't want that, not that I don't want it either."

"How do you mean?"

"I mean that stardom isn't the reason I'm doing this. Not to sound arrogant, but as long as I get to make the music I like and some people enjoy it, it doesn't matter how many or how few do. There's no greater feeling of fulfillment than when I've made someone happy through what I do. Those are the kinds of moments I want to keep accumulating in my life."

Shuichi was stunned.

In his line of work, the people he'd encountered, colleagues and clients, were hyper-focused on income, insurance, and plans, and lived under the assumption that they needed a certain standard of income to get by. Rarely did he encounter anyone who made ends meet on his modest income doing what he loved like the man before him.

His greatest shock, however, wasn't that the young man managed to lead such a lifestyle but that he seemed happy doing it.

Whether the man was happy wasn't a certainty. But Shuichi felt confident that the man was in the kind of mood the driver had described. At the very least, surely he was able to control his moods. Shuichi felt a shiver run through him.

The strength of character in this man . . .

After finishing his beer, Shuichi ordered a whisky with water.

He then said, "I'd sure like to have a listen."

Relaxing his lips into a smile, the man reached into his bag at his feet, took out a CD, and extended his hand toward Shuichi, setting it on the counter. Shuichi stood up, walked over, and taking the CD, sat down next to him.

The CD's jacket cover featured a black-and-white profile image of the man and the name "Arata," written in English.

"Arata-san . . ."

"My name is Arata Fujikami, but I go by 'Arata' written in the English alphabet. You're welcome to it if you'd like."

"Oh, no. Please let me buy it. I'm happy to pay."

Shuichi turned the CD case over and found "1,500 yen" printed on the back.

"Take it, please. I only take money from people who've heard and liked my music. And, you . . ."

"Okada." Shuichi hastily introduced himself.

"Okada-san, you haven't heard my music yet."

Shuichi decided to accept his kindness.

"In that case, I'll take you up on your offer. I'll listen to it when I get home."

With gratitude, he raised the CD to his forehead with both his hands. The bartender set the whisky and water in front of him. Taking a sip from the glass, he turned to Fujikami.

"So, aren't your days tough? I mean, you have no idea what your income is going to be tomorrow, much less the next month. Doesn't that scare you?"

The question was a sincere one. Although the thought of making a living by doing what you loved certainly sounded cool, committing to such a lifestyle required resolve. There was no guarantee of a future, much less tomorrow.

Yet the man in front of him, who lived exactly such a lifestyle, didn't show the least bit of desperation. Not only that, being able to come here with the earnings from doing what he loved, he said, brought him joy.

Perhaps it was his youth talking or a lack of deep contemplation. Nevertheless, the young man's boldness and resilience were qualities that Shuichi lacked. When it came to the future, Shuichi was always anxious. It had always been like that since childhood. Shuichi couldn't envision himself living like this man.

Shuichi was tempted to ask if Fujikami was ever anxious about the future but, not wanting to be rude, decided against it. If Shuichi were in Fujikami's shoes, he'd probably be worried sick.

Fujikami took a sip from his drink, grinning. "Have you played the guitar before, Okada-san?"

"Never, I'm afraid."

"Well, if you play long enough, this is what happens, see?"

He held out his left hand. Shuichi eyed the hand intently but couldn't understand what he was getting at.

"The fingers get callused."

He seemed to be inviting him to touch them, so Shuichi felt the ends of Fujikami's fingers.

"You're right."

"If you ever have a chance, try picking up a guitar. At first, it's hard to produce a good sound. Your fingers are still soft, so when you try to hold down the strings, it's your fingers that get compressed. The tension on the strings is surprisingly tight, so you have to press down on them pretty hard to produce a sound. And when you do, all the other parts of your fingers that you think aren't touching the strings get in the way."

"Why don't you give it a try? There's no one else in the bar but us right now. Go right ahead," said the bartender at the other end of the counter with a smile.

"Oh, I . . ."

Before Shuichi could decline the offer, Fujikami opened the guitar case, took out the guitar, and handed it to him.

It was the first time he was handling a guitar. He cradled it gingerly in his arms.

"Try strumming the strings with your right hand," Fujikami said.

Shuichi tentatively ran his fingers across the six strings. Instead of the smooth chord he hoped for, what came out was the sparse sound of six detached notes.

"Wow, you're right. The strings are tight."

"Would you like to try with the left hand?"

Fujikami directed Shuichi, indicating where to press with each finger one by one.

"This is a C chord. That's it. Now, keep your left hand where it is and try strumming with your right hand again."

"O-okay."

Doing as instructed, Shuichi ran his fingers across the strings, but only one string issued a sound, while the others failed to produce a clear tone.

"Ha, this is harder than I thought!"

He reset his fingers several times and tried to play the C chord but couldn't manage it. Laughing to cover his embarrassment, Shuichi returned the guitar to Fujikami.

"Keep at it and your fingers will toughen up, like

this. And after your fingers get callused, you'll be able to hold down the strings with a touch like so," Fujikami explained, demonstrating the C chord with a crash.

Shuichi had pressed so firmly on the strings that his fingers were tingling. Fujikami quickly stowed away the guitar in its case.

"You can play the guitar because your fingers toughen up. Don't you think that's amazing?"

"Amazing?" Shuichi frowned.

"Yes, with persistence, your body adapts to the guitar. And it's not just a guitar. If the human body continues to do one thing consistently, it will gradually transform into a shape that's best suited for the task. Amazing, right?"

Shuichi had never thought of it as amazing before, but now that he did, it was quite extraordinary.

"I believe that every part of the human body starts flexible so that it can easily adapt. And when you start using your body for a particular task and work at it, the necessary parts toughen up and grow suited to that task. But there's always something that accompanies that process."

"Something that accompanies . . ." Shuichi looked down at his fingers, swollen and red.

"That's right. Pain. It's only with pain that the body adapts to a form that's suitable for the task. Being soft is proof that you can adapt for anything and it's through experiencing pain that you can become a specialist."

"Pain, huh?" Shuichi listened intently, his fingers still throbbing.

"Why must humans wear shoes when animals can roam around mountains without wearing anything on their feet? I think the same holds true in this case too. It's because our feet have been protected by shoes and socks since birth, so the backs of our feet have grown accustomed to that. It isn't that our feet are soft and weak but that humans have been overprotective of them."

"Overprotective?" Shuichi let slip a grin, amused by the expression.

"Yes, we've been wearing shoes to avoid feeling pain. But if we quit wearing them and overcome the initial pain, in time, we'll develop feet that have no need for shoes."

"No need for shoes . . ."

Fujikami laughed. "Although, I doubt anyone wants that. Anyway, it was just an example."

"Uh-huh," answered Shuichi, like he didn't understand entirely.

"In essence, all humans are soft and weak in the beginning. But if they keep working at it, despite the pain that comes with it, they get stronger and tougher. By the time they no longer feel pain, they've transformed to fit the task at hand. That's my theory anyway."

"I see."

"That applies to my life too. Opening my guitar case, performing my songs, and making a living from it is quite hard. But I thought that was the only way forward to recondition my weak and anxious self."

"You were . . . anxious?"

"Believe it or not, I used to be a salaryman."

"You were?"

"You know the doormats that you usually find at store entrances? The ones you wipe your shoes on. My job was to go around replacing them. I dreamt of earning a living with my music, of course, but I just couldn't bring myself to take the plunge. The job was supposed to be a way to finance my music career, but deep down, I was afraid of losing that steady salary. I was a coward."

"That's probably true of anyone. After all, you need a livelihood to embark on a challenge. You're certainly not a coward, Arata-san. You can't perform in front of a crowd being a coward."

Fujikami shook his head. "I was terrified of performing in front of an audience. At first, my fingers would tremble and if I stumbled midway through, my mind would go blank, and I couldn't continue playing. I never stumbled practicing at home but couldn't play in front of an audience . . . that's how it was in the beginning. It was then that I realized . . ."

"That pain is a requirement of becoming stronger?" Shuichi interjected.

"Yes, I realized that I was fearful and anxious and that I had to toughen up. And for that to happen, pain was a necessary part of the process. And as I continued busking on the street, I came to embrace the trials and tribulations. In time, I learned to play in front of an audience without stumbling and sought out new challenges. Before long, I quit my job. I thought that when this challenge no longer felt painful, I would truly have the strength to live and be free."

"And?" Shuichi asked with some anticipation. "Are you stronger now?"

Fujikami grinned. "I don't know. But I can say that I no longer worry over this and that when something happens. It's a strange thing. When I had a lot, I used to obsess over things like that constantly, but now living in a tiny, rundown apartment with my guitar as my only companion, I hardly think about it."

"Oh?"

"So, I guess I am stronger."

"Then, you'll go on busking until someday . . ."

Fujikami shook his head. "I'm not sure about that. What I can tell you now is that this life is definitely toughening me up. I feel as if I can do anything from here on out. I can continue playing music, launch a company, or start a store. Recently, I've come to think that you can accomplish just about anything if you make yourself strong for it."

"I see . . ."

"You asked if not knowing whether I have a secure income tomorrow was tough. My answer is that it is. But I chose this life wanting this challenge, so it doesn't scare me."

"So you'll become stronger and tougher . . ."

"That's right. So I plan to keep challenging myself for a while. But occasionally, it's important to give yourself a break, which is why . . ." With that, Fujikami raised his glass.

"Which is why you're here." Finishing the thought, Shuichi raised his glass.

"WHY MATSUYAMA ALL OF A SUDDEN?"

These were the first words out of Yuko's mouth on the other end of the phone.

"I'll explain when I get back. It was work related," Shuichi mumbled, struggling to come up with a convincing excuse. "Listen, there's something I've been meaning to ask you."

"What is it?"

"It's about the meeting with Yumeka's homeroom teacher yesterday."

"Yeah?"

"You two seemed to be discussing something when I got there. What were you talking about?"

"We were just chatting, I think. Wait, oh, that's right. You happened to come up in the conversation, and when I mentioned that you sell insurance, he said that he was thinking about taking out an insurance policy and that he wanted to talk. I suggested that he talk to you after the meeting, but then your mood soured . . ."

"Okay, thanks."

Shuichi ended the call. Yuko's revelation came as

no surprise. He'd assumed that was the conversation that Yuko and the teacher were having ever since the driver told him about it, and Yuko's statement just now confirmed it.

Everything the driver said was true.

If that were the case, it would mean that something had to have happened to improve his luck at the bar that day.

Yet he didn't have the feeling that anything significant had changed. He had the experience of going to a bar alone for the first time, and the words of the musician he'd met there had resonated with him, of that he was certain.

But he hadn't discussed his work, and though he'd given Fujikami his card before parting, he'd only had the casual intention of introducing his name rather than business purposes. He understood that Fujikami wasn't someone to whom he could recommend life insurance nor did he see any sign of securing a new contract elsewhere. The driver had mentioned the possibility of a future where he would find happiness by quitting his insurance job. In which case, could there have been a sign to pursue another path? If there were . . .

The guitar . . . ?

Shuichi grimaced at the mere thought of it.

No way a middle-aged man north of forty is going to pick up the guitar and become a musician.

And yet contemplating a future that wasn't an extension of the current situation made Shuichi's heart dance. The thrill was palpable even to him.

But every time that he felt that way, he suspected he was escaping reality, so he pulled his thoughts back to pondering a future that was an extension of his current situation, knowing that what awaited him there was unavoidable suffering.

I'm not pulling in any contracts. What am I doing here?

One part of him blamed himself. At the same time, another part of him was beginning to think that, like Arata-san, he needed more challenges to stop fearing for the future. Shuichi's heart was beginning to edge away from the brink of despair. He recalled what the driver had said. Perhaps when he looked back on his life later, he would come to see that night's events as a turning point. Though his anxiety remained, Shuichi also began to embrace a dim hope for the future.

EARLY THE NEXT MORNING, SHUICHI TRAVELED to an inn at Dogo Hot Springs. He intended to take a long soak in the baths and take some time to sort out his present circumstances.

A client who was from Matsuyama had once told him that Dogo was a place Prince Shotoku had visited for its curative benefits centuries ago. Whenever your mind was spinning from all the troubles coming at you at once, relaxation was key. It was with that in mind that he spent the night at an inn.

As soon as he got out of the bath and put on a yukata, beads of sweat began to coat his body. The gentle morning breeze passing through the damp yukata felt indescribably refreshing. He hadn't had such a pleasant morning in a long while.

Later, after changing back into the suit he'd been wearing since the day before, Shuichi took the streetcar to wander Okaido, a shopping district of Matsuyama. The streets were teeming with activity, and the stroll lifted his spirits.

Hey, it's not so hard to keep up a good mood!

The moment the thought crossed his mind, he found himself in front of a music store. He went inside as if he were magnetically pulled in.

He didn't think anyone would believe his state of mind at that moment, especially since he didn't believe it himself. He exited the music store with a guitar case slung over his shoulder. When he tried, in his own way, to analyze what possessed him to purchase a guitar, the only conclusion he could draw was that the driver's words had guided him to it.

If he had indeed been visited by a turning point at that bar the day before and if his good mood was supposed to allow him to sense it, then the answer could only lead to the guitar. Furthermore, the fact that he happened upon a music shop, despite not looking for one, seemed like a sign.

He found the same brand of guitar that Fujikami played. It was called a Martin, and he was shocked at how expensive it was. The staff worker suggested that if he was going to buy a guitar, he might as well invest in an expensive one. However, the Martin was far beyond his budget. In the end, he settled on a guitar for about one hundred thousand yen and, afterward, still regretted making such an extravagant purchase. It was still about a tenth of the price of the Martin.

It's something I need right now.

Of this he was certain. But as for how or why he needed it, that wasn't something he could explain satisfactorily to anyone, much less to himself. It was after he'd made the purchase that he wondered for the first time, *How am I going to explain this to Yuko?*

The thought made him roll his eyes.

Her first reaction would likely be to angrily ask, *What in the world did you buy?*

She wouldn't yell, but she would certainly complain in her usual way:

For starters, how are you even able to afford it?

You're just going to quit anyway, and then the guitar will go in the trash.

But once she had her say, she would pull an apologetic look as if she'd said too much and say, *Look, I understand sometimes you have to make purchases like these to maintain business relationships*, and there the conversation would end.

But that was under the condition that work was going smoothly. What Shuichi had to tell her afterward would create a confusing situation for Yuko, one that she would find difficult to wrap her mind around.

I had twenty contracts canceled.

Next month's paycheck could be cut by a third. Maybe even by half.

I'm going to have to return ten months' worth of salary.

The sum will also be deducted from future bonuses, so we can't expect a bonus for a while.

If we have to pay it out of our savings, we may need to dip into Yumeka's high school fund.

So that's why we won't be able to go on the Paris trip.

None of these he could say lightheartedly, and each one required quite a bit of preparation on the listener's part too, but as things stood now, Shuichi found himself in a position where he would have to say all of these things.

Even if Yuko begrudgingly accepted the situation, she would surely ask, *Then why did you buy a guitar at a time like this?*

Why? Because that's what I'm supposed to do. You see, I've been getting signs that opportunities will open up in the future if I buy a guitar now.

There was no way she would be satisfied with such an answer. Then, what if he told her about the mysterious driver?

Shuichi shook his head, knowing she wouldn't believe that either.

WHEN HE RETURNED HOME AFTER DARK, YUKO'S REaction was different from what he was expecting. As soon as she saw the guitar on his shoulder, her eyes widened in shock, and after a moment of speechlessness, she managed to squeeze out, "W-what did you buy?"

Despite the predictable reaction, he didn't detect any anger in her expression. Only surprise.

"It's complicated. I'll explain later," he answered evasively, but Yuko didn't seem particularly angry, nor did she demand an explanation.

Did she think he had bought it to maintain a client relationship? Or that his boss was forcing him to learn the guitar to perform at the year-end company party?

Whatever the case, she seemed to have accepted that he had some extenuating reason for purchasing the guitar without further explanation.

Shuichi breathed a momentary sigh of relief, but the biggest issue remained unresolved. He still couldn't bring himself to confess what he needed to say.

IS EFFORT ALWAYS REWARDED?

Rocked by the taxi's movement, Shuichi looked out the window at the scenery, rubbing his thumb against the fingertips that had become slightly callused from his late-night guitar practices. He'd assumed the strange taxi driver would come every day, but five days had passed since the driver had last appeared. *Maybe it was all just a dream*, he thought. As the line between dream and reality began to blur, the taxi driver appeared before him.

As usual, the driver set off on the road without announcing their destination. Shuichi sat silently in the back seat, pondering the changes that had transpired over the past few days.

Stay positive. He had put the driver's teachings into practice, hoping that it would improve his sensor to catch luck-changing opportunities and transform his life. He had hoped that by doing so, a turning point in his life would come upon him, but in these past few days, there hadn't been any noticeable changes.

Since he last parted with the driver, Shuichi had not secured a single new contract. With payday creeping ever closer and backed into a corner as he was, it felt as if his luck was getting worse rather than better. Whenever he found himself thinking, *I don't have time for this* or *What am I to do?* he smoothed out the wrinkles between his brows and reminded himself to keep his spirits up. That was his daily struggle.

Even now, staring out the window, he couldn't help but feel unsatisfied, anxious even, about the lack of change in his life despite maintaining a positive mood. Still, he kept on telling himself to stay cheerful or he might miss the signs.

Shuichi also had a nagging feeling that he was forgetting something important. It wasn't until he caught a look at the driver's face in the mirror that he remembered what it was.

The rewards card . . .

The first discussion he'd had with the driver was about points.

The driver had said that, like points on a rewards card, luck wasn't inherently good or bad but about whether you used it or saved it. So, if something good happened to you, it wasn't necessarily because you had good luck but because you chose to use the luck you'd saved up. At that moment, a thought flickered into his head:

That would mean nothing good would happen if you didn't save up your luck beforehand.

On the other hand, the driver had also taught him that if he didn't maintain a cheerful mood, his internal sensor for sensing lucky opportunities wouldn't work.

As Shuichi recalled each of the driver's teachings, it dawned upon him that he might have been misunderstanding something fundamental, and he nearly gasped aloud.

Now, wait. The driver said that keeping your spirits up would improve the sensor's ability to sense lucky opportunities, but he didn't say that you would save any luck. If luck works like points you save on a rewards card, then that would mean even if I was in a good mood and sensed an opportunity, I wouldn't have any luck to use if I haven't been saving it up throughout my life.

Could he unequivocally say that he'd been saving up his luck to conjure enough to transform his life?

The answer was no.

In which case, even if he did maintain a cheerful mood and managed to detect a luck-changing opportunity, the resulting luck would inevitably be small. Shuichi sat up, grabbing the seat back in front of him.

"Is something the matter?" The startled driver looked at Shuichi through the rearview mirror.

"Tell me something. You said the luck sensor doesn't work unless you're in a good mood, right?"

"Yes, that's right."

"Being in a good mood only lets you sense luck-changing opportunities, but it doesn't lead to accumulating luck, does it?"

"That's not true. You can accumulate luck just by living every day with a good spirit."

Shuichi leaned back in his seat, looking somewhat relieved. "Oh."

"Yes, even dust, if piled up, can become a mountain."

"Dust?" Shuichi couldn't keep himself from leaning forward again.

"Yes, but it's nothing to sneeze at. Over a year, the difference in accumulated luck between someone who spends every day cheerfully and someone who lives in a perpetually sour mood is huge and insurmountable."

"Yeah, that figures." Shuichi slumped back in his seat, disappointed.

Had Shuichi been living in a positive mood since childhood, the luck he would have accumulated would have been enormous by now, but he'd only started applying himself to be cheerful a few days ago. In which case, he would only have accumulated a mere speck of luck. It was unrealistic to expect enough of it to secure a miraculous contract within the next few days.

"Never mind the dust. Isn't there some way to accumulate a mountain of luck from the get-go?"

Shuichi meant to mumble this complaint to himself, but the driver, keeping his eyes trained on the road, answered, "There is."

A spark returned to Shuichi's eyes.

"There is?"

"There is."

"What do I do? Tell me."

"Use your time for the happiness of others."

"Use my time for the happiness of others." Shuichi could do little more than repeat the driver's words.

"Right, but there's more. You spend time for the sake of someone's happiness, and by doing so, you also gain something. The difference between what you did for someone versus what they did for you is luck."

"What you did for someone versus what they did

for you is . . . luck? How do you mean?" Shuichi asked, unable to fully grasp the driver's meaning.

"It isn't complicated."

The driver changed lanes to pass a stationary moving truck.

"Let's say that you take one of your days off to help a friend move. You would be using your time for someone's happiness. Now, let's say that after you've finished moving, your friend treats you to a nice unagi dinner as thanks."

Just then, they drove past an unagi restaurant.

"What you did for someone was help them move, and what they did for you was treat you to an unagi dinner. Well? Do you think you've done too much for them? Or do you think they've done too much for you?"

"Hmm, seems about right."

"Okay. Then it's safe to assume that no luck was used or saved in this case. But what if that friend were to give you two hundred thousand yen as a thank-you gift?"

"That's way too much."

"Right, in which case you could assume that you spent your luck. On the other hand, if there wasn't any gesture of gratitude . . ."

"That would mean I saved my luck."

"Exactly."

The driver's explanation was as clear as day. So, that was how luck accumulated!

"Then if you go above and beyond for someone and they do nothing in return, you stand to accumulate quite a bit of luck. Do I have that right?"

"You do."

Folding his arms across his chest, Shuichi stared at the back of the passenger-side headrest. The part of him that was convinced and another part of him that wasn't continued to debate each other in his head.

For a while he stayed that way, his expression clouded with doubt, until he let out a contemplative groan and said, "Does the same hold true with work?"

The driver's face brightened as if he'd read Shuichi's mind. He met Shuichi's gaze through the mirror. "Yes, it does."

"That sounds like a losing scenario."

"How so?"

"In a moving job, you're probably going to make ten thousand yen for a day's work. If you only get five thousand yen after working that much, you'd be at a loss."

"No, you wouldn't. You would be saving that much in luck."

"That kind of thinking is going to get you exploited by companies and cause you to lose your entire life."

The driver shook his head. "That won't happen. People like that will go on accumulating luck, until one day—"

This time, it was Shuichi who shook his head.

"No, that can't be true. Can you honestly say beyond a shadow of a doubt that will happen? God knows there are any number of people whose lives don't go that way. All they do is get used and end their lives without a single good thing happening to them. And you expect me to believe you?"

The driver cracked a crooked smile. "Most of those people would have had the chance to use up the luck they'd saved until then if they had just maintained a better mood. The people you're talking about, Okada-san? Most of them go about their lives without any semblance of cheerfulness." The driver gestured out the window with a nod.

Outside was the entrance to a train station from which a steady stream of people was pouring out. None of their faces showed any sign of cheerfulness.

The driver did have a point. And it wasn't just the people outside. The people he would pass during his commute, himself included, all looked as if their unhappiness was a given. Was the driver saying that even those people could encounter a turning point in their lives if they'd just be in good spirits? Could he honestly say that for everyone?

Wait . . .

Shuichi played back the driver's previous words in his head.

"You said *most* people."

The driver shot Shuichi a sincere grin. "You're very sharp on the details."

"Don't give me that. In my line of work, if you're not attentive to the tiniest nuances in language, you're liable to run into trouble later. Never mind that. By saying *most* people, you're admitting that not everyone can use the luck they've saved."

"Now, don't get excited. What I'm saying is, yes, but definitely not."

"Hunh? What are you saying?"

Suddenly, Shuichi felt his blood boil.

"There you go getting irritated again." The driver chuckled and admonished Shuichi, appearing not the least bit flustered.

"Yes, but definitely not? Who in their right mind would accept that as an answer? You're not making sense."

The driver burst out laughing. "I guess you're right about that."

"This isn't funny! I've done things that are completely out of my comfort zone and stayed positive like an idiot because I trusted you."

"Yes, you even bought a guitar and practiced every night," added the driver.

"That's right—hey, are you mocking me?"

"It's just that you're so testy. I thought I'd lighten the mood."

"This isn't a laughing matter. Now you owe me a proper explanation."

Keeping his hands on the wheel, the driver shrugged. "All right. I might as well tell you, since it's about time we discussed this anyway."

"Tell me what?"

"Have you ever thought about why I showed up in my taxi in front of you, Okada-san?"

"What?" Shuichi was lost for words.

"My job is to take you somewhere you will encounter a luck-changing opportunity that will change your life. Plus, you get to ride all you want until this meter hits zero. Don't you think that's an incredible service?"

Come to think of it, the driver was right. Just having the luxury of tens of thousands of yen worth of free taxi rides was something to be grateful for. Yet here he was not only failing to show any gratitude but also venting his anger at the driver. When he realized he was acting like a selfish child, his anger quickly gave way to embarrassment. His back felt hot with shame.

"Listen, I'm grateful to you, I am," he said a bit contritely.

"Are you? Happy to hear it. But have you ever given thought to why you're my passenger?"

Shuichi shook his head in silence.

Unable to tell whether the driver had seen his response or not, he answered quietly, "No, I haven't."

"Well, then, think about it. Why do you think I showed up before you?"

"That's—"

Shuichi started to say that he was lucky to be chosen but stopped himself. Luck wasn't good or bad but something to use or save. It was the driver who had told him that. No, luck couldn't possibly be the answer. In which case, the answer had to be that he was chosen because he'd accumulated enough luck; however, he couldn't recall ever living a life where he accumulated enough luck to be chosen for something so special. The last time he remembered being cheerful was probably back in grade school. By the time he was in junior high school, being in a perpetually bad mood had become his default state, and it had stayed that way for well over thirty-five years. He couldn't possibly claim to have accumulated any luck himself.

"I don't know," Shuichi answered honestly, his voice now calmer. He then asked in earnest, "Tell me. Why did you choose me as your passenger?"

THE TASTE OF SOBA

"Isn't it about time you went to bed, dear?"

"Hm? Yeah . . ." Masafumi gave Tamiko an absentminded reply, his attention fixed on the store's ledger, bankbook, and stacks of documents.

He'd noticed the store's sales gradually declining about two years ago, but he hadn't anticipated sales to drop so sharply in the last year.

"We should speak to Shuichi and tell him we'll

need to cut down on his allowance starting next month," suggested Tamiko. "He mentioned that he increased his hours at his part-time job."

Masafumi parted his firmly set lips just long enough to grunt, "We're not telling him," before crossing his arms again and returning his gaze to the ledger. The reality before him was undeniable.

I can't make the payments.

No matter how hard he looked, he simply didn't have the money.

One more year . . .

In his mind, he counted down the days until his son, Shuichi, would graduate from university.

Despite sending Shuichi a monthly allowance, he couldn't claim he was providing his son with enough to concentrate solely on his studies while living in the city. Shuichi still needed to work part-time to make ends meet. While he'd probably taken extra shifts because he needed the money to go out, it was only natural for a university student to need a little spending money for fun. Masafumi's paternal pride simply didn't allow him to cut back on his son's allowance because his son was working more hours.

He wanted his son to lead a different, easier life than he had. To achieve this, he hoped for Shuichi to graduate from university and get a job in the city. That wish alone was the driving force that kept him getting up in the morning despite his financial struggles.

The same banks that had practically said, "We'll lend you as much as you need," a few years ago had completely changed their tune, which made securing any kind of loan difficult. Considering his current age and the shop's declining sales over the last few years, he knew that borrowing funds to keep the shop running would be a challenge. Not only that but the economic downturn triggered by the collapse of the bubble two years ago also loomed over Masafumi's life in the form of reluctant banks.

Nevertheless, he might have been able to borrow something if he were willing to extend the repayment period and continue working well into old age, but since he still had outstanding debts from the "we'll lend you as much as you need" days, the notion of taking out more loans was unthinkable.

Thinking back on it now, he didn't understand why he had borrowed such a sum in the first place. It was as if he'd blindly assumed that if the banks were willing to lend him the money, then he must be capable of paying it back.

With the land value of the shopping district continuing to decline, even if he were to sell the shop along with the house on top of it, there would still be debts remaining.

"We're going to have to cut back on costs where we can and ride it out somehow."

The solution was painfully obvious. Precious few places were left where cuts could be made. The most recent expense he'd had to let go of was his golf club membership. He'd paid an exorbitant amount for it, believing that its value would only appreciate, but when it came time to sell, its value had decreased tenfold.

From the disrepair of the shopping arcade to the plummeting value of the golf club membership, Masafumi had not anticipated such hard times. He sifted through the stacks of documents on the table and picked up an envelope. An insurance policy.

The life insurance he'd acquired before Shuichi was born increased its premiums steadily along with the insured's age. As Shuichi grew older, the need for a large payout decreased, prompting periodic reviews of the policy. Nevertheless, Masafumi continued to pay the premiums, thinking it necessary until Shuichi graduated from university. That wasn't the only reason, however. Should Masafumi ever become ill or require treatment, he didn't want to burden the family and potentially rob Shuichi of his future. It was a scenario he desperately wanted to avoid.

Masafumi took a long look at the insurance policy.

"I WOULD HAVE PACKED YOU LUNCH IF YOU TOLD me yesterday," Tamiko said as Masafumi sat on the entrance steps, tying his shoes.

"It's okay. I'll grab something on the way," he replied, getting up and lifting the rucksack on his shoulders.

Wearing the shoes and clothes he'd bought to

go hiking with Shuichi when his son was little, he turned around and offered a gentle smile to Tamiko. She was momentarily taken by surprise by the gesture but returned the smile.

"What time shall I expect you back?"

"Gee, I don't know. I haven't been hiking in a while. That depends on how well my body holds up."

"Don't overdo it, okay?"

"Okay."

With that, Masafumi stepped out the door. It wasn't every day that Masafumi smiled at her, and Tamiko couldn't help but smile herself after the door closed.

"I wonder what's got into him," she muttered to herself before heading into the kitchen to fix herself breakfast. It was 6:00 a.m.

"I GUESS MY HIKE STARTS HERE."

After glancing back at the store, which was shuttered for the holiday, Masafumi turned back around and began to walk. As he made his way through the

THE LUCKY RIDE

shopping arcade, then out onto the street in front of the train station, a taxi approached from the right, stopped in front of him, and popped open the rear door.

Meeting the driver's gaze, Masafumi said gently, "I'm not looking for a ride."

"Get in. The ride has already been paid for."

Taken by the driver's words and guileless smile, Masafumi climbed into the back seat. He considered asking what the driver meant by "paid for," but he wasn't one to bother over the details. If the driver was telling him to get in, that was good enough for him.

Not worth worrying about today, he decided and didn't give it another moment's thought. The driver set the taxi in motion without asking for a destination.

Masafumi listened to the driver's story in silence all through the journey. The more the driver spoke, the more peculiar and outlandish the story became, but Masafumi didn't feel the urge to question or seek clarification on any of the details. He wasn't paying much attention at all. As he observed the fare meter tick down from 100,000 to 98,820, he muttered, in a detached tone, "What a strange job."

The taxi rumbled down a road running parallel to a river, against the current. They were heading toward the mountains. Masafumi hadn't mentioned a specific destination, but the driver must have assumed it from Masafumi's attire. The mountains on the other side of the river drew closer, indicating they were nearing the trails to the mountain peaks.

The moment Masafumi was about to tell the driver to let him off up ahead, the driver turned on the blinker and veered right off the road.

"Hey? Where do you think you're going?" Masafumi asked.

The driver didn't answer.

Eventually, they pulled up in front of an old traditional Japanese house with several banners fluttering out front.

Turning around, the driver smiled and asked, "The soba here is like nothing you've ever tasted. Wouldn't you like to try it?"

Masafumi grimaced and shook his head. "I'm not looking for a meal right now. Would you mind turning back?"

"No," the driver said firmly.

"No?"

"That's right, no. Even if you don't plan on waking up tomorrow, your last meal is going to be the soba here."

Masafumi's eyes widened in bewilderment. The driver had an uncanny ability to read his thoughts. His expression tense, Masafumi fixed a look at the driver, who was gazing right at him.

Unfazed by Masafumi's expression, the young driver continued, "I don't care where you go or what you do after that. But first, you're going to try the soba at this shop."

"Why are you insisting that I eat here?" His voice trembled. He was unsettled by the feeling that the driver knew his intentions.

"Because today is the anniversary of Ryozo-san's death."

"What . . . did you . . ." Masafumi heard himself gasp. "How would you know that?" he asked, barely able to conceal his shock, but the driver ignored the question.

"July 7, 1944, is the day your father, Ryozo-san, died. He perished on the island of Saipan. You were only a year old, so you couldn't have known how happy he was when you were born or how much he adored you. You don't even have a memory of him, I bet. But even if you might have forgotten, Ryozo-san loved you very much. He died wishing only for your future happiness."

MASAFUMI GREW UP HEARING ALMOST NOTHING about his biological father. The father he knew was the man his mother remarried after the war, and that father had a child from another marriage. Thus, Masafumi grew up with a stepbrother and a younger half sister who was born to his mother and stepfather. His mother had told him about the family situation when he was old enough to understand such matters, but sensing, even as a child, that he shouldn't talk about his biological father, he refrained from asking his mother any questions.

Though his mother had told him that his father's name was Ryozo and that he'd died in the war, Masafumi had no way of knowing when or where his father had died. Not even his mother knew the exact date of his death. Since none of the soldiers who had been deployed with Ryozo returned, it was understandable that such information wasn't readily available.

"Is what you say . . . true? Did my father die in Saipan?"

"Yes, at 6:12 a.m. The exact time you boarded this taxi. Ryozo-san, or shall I say, all of the surviving soldiers, including him, had gone without food for over ten days when the final assault took place. They had rifles but they had long since run out of ammunition. The only weapons they had in their possession were the bent bayonets affixed to their rifles. Some of the soldiers had only rocks to use as weapons. It was under these conditions that they made their final charge, running toward the tens of thousands of enemy soldiers who relentlessly attacked them in tanks and fighter planes.

"On July 6, the night before he passed away, there was an exceptionally beautiful sunset on Saipan Island. At the time, one surviving soldier said to your father, 'I would have liked to have eaten Akafuku one last time.' The soldier was from Ise and Akafuku mochi was one of his favorite childhood treats. He wanted to share this memory with someone before he died. Then, Ryozo-san remarked that the soba in his hometown was delicious because of the water quality in those parts. It was the best soba around. Upon hearing this, the soldier remarked, 'You must be longing for that soba one last time, I bet.' And then your father shook his head. 'I have a newborn son. If he's around to enjoy it, that's all that matters. I'll die tomorrow so he can live to eat that soba one day.'"

THE LUCKY RIDE

Masafumi listened to the driver's story, his mouth slightly ajar. Tears fell from his unblinking eyes.

"Would you like to hear more?"

Having been absorbed in the driver's story and barely registering a reaction, Masafumi suddenly came back to himself and responded, "Tell me, please." He leaned forward in his seat, bringing his face closer to the driver's.

"Then let's go inside. I'm happy to tell you over some soba." With that, the driver popped open the rear door.

Masafumi wiped his eyes and stepped out of the taxi.

MASAFUMI STARED INTENTLY AT THE SOBA NOO-dles brought to him.

The white noodles piled on top of the bamboo tray glistened with the unmistakable sheen of having just been rinsed in cold water.

Masafumi had grown up in poverty for much of

his childhood. His mother used to speak of how tirelessly she worked so they would never go hungry.

By the time Masafumi graduated from junior high school, he had never experienced a single instance that made him feel that hunger. Gradually, over time, he was able to eat as much as he wanted whenever he wanted, and that became the norm.

LOOKING BACK ON HIS LIFE, MASAFUMI REALIZED for the first time that perhaps the reason he never wanted for a meal was due to Ryozo's unwavering determination.

"Let's dig in before the noodles get soft," said the driver, offering Masafumi some chopsticks.

"Right." Taking the chopsticks from the driver, he gazed at the soba, put his hands together in front of his face in gratitude, and bowed. "*Itadakimasu.*"

As he attempted to dip the noodles in the sauce, his hands trembled uncontrollably, tears streaming down his face.

"Wait . . . I can't." He set his chopsticks down and covered his face with his hand.

The driver took out a handkerchief and offered it to him. "Are you all right?"

"I'm sorry. This is the soba my father wanted me to eat?"

"Yes. This shop has been here for a very long time. Ryozo-san was fond of the noodles here."

"I've eaten my fill of anything I desired and taken it for granted. But my father . . . I wish he could have eaten this one last time . . ."

Masafumi's sobbing became so intense that he could no longer speak.

"I understand how you feel. That's why you should have it for him, Okada-san."

Masafumi nodded emphatically several times, sniffled, and picked up the chopsticks again. Though his hands still trembled, he took a larger portion of soba than before, quickly dipped it in the sauce, and slurped it into his mouth.

He nodded again and again, chewing on the noodles. There were no words, only tears. He continued to nod long after he swallowed the soba in his mouth.

He was having a conversation with his father. The driver decided not to say anything more. He quickly finished his soba and stood up, saying, "I'll wait for you in the car."

Masafumi responded with a smile.

IT WAS WELL OVER AN HOUR LATER WHEN MASAfumi emerged from the shop and returned to the taxi parked outside.

He seemed to have had a good conversation with his father. When he got in the car, his eyes were red from crying, but he looked a great deal refreshed, as though a weight had been lifted from his shoulders.

The driver closed the rear door and started driving. They traced their path back along the mountain road by the river. Masafumi said nothing. The driver said he knew where to go. Although Masafumi didn't know where he was being taken, he knew that the mountains were no longer where he needed to go. Masafumi didn't insist on going to the mountains either.

After they traveled for a while in silence, Masafumi said, "Did you know why I was going to the mountains today?"

"Yes, you were planning to slip and take a little fall."

Masafumi chuckled. "You really do know everything, don't you? And you showed up to stop me?"

"No, I didn't necessarily intend to stop you. My only job was to take you to the soba shop."

"I see. Well, thanks. Thanks to you, my mind is made. Somewhere along the line, I got so used to living a comfortable life that I lost the vitality, or maybe it's called the hunger, to survive."

The driver didn't offer a response, merely smiling back through the rearview mirror. Masafumi then began to tell him his life story.

"UNTIL RECENTLY, MY LIFE TRULY HAS BEEN SMOOTH sailing, as if my impoverished childhood was a dream. The store thrived on the wave of postwar recovery, and when I took it over, the shopping district was established, and by sheer luck, the shop ended up in the best spot smack in the middle of the arcade. The money kept coming in without my having to do a thing. I lived a comfortable life untouched by hunger. I would frequent hostess bars at night and, on days off, shoot some rounds with my golfing buddies from the shopping street.

"When the money was rolling in, the bank eagerly lent me more. And when I used the loan to renovate the shop, sales increased again. I have never worried about my future. Considering my childhood, I truly believed we were born in fortunate times. Before I knew it, I became accustomed to that lifestyle.

"But in the past year or two, there was a sudden shift in the tides. Gradually, people began to disappear from the shopping arcade, and many of the shop owners shuttered their stores due to declining income and old age. Everything would have been fine if new businesses moved in, but they couldn't because the back end of the shops and the second floor are used as residences. In an instant, the shopping district became deserted. By the time I realized this could be serious, there was nothing I could do. People had already drifted toward the shopping malls. No matter what I did, I couldn't redirect the flow of people back to the shop. It made me question why this was happening to me. I thought it was all bad luck.

"After eating the soba, I sat awhile and started thinking that when everything was going well, maybe it wasn't that I was lucky but that I'd been using the luck that someone else had saved up.

"I'm willing to bet that my biological father died without ever having experienced anything that would make him consider himself to be lucky in any way, as I have. Of course, it wasn't just my father. It's probably true of everyone who lived through that era, including the people who perished on Saipan Island, as you mentioned earlier. We've been living off the luck they had saved for us, and I started to feel that maybe that luck had run out.

"The same holds for why you showed up in front

of me. You didn't come because of anything I did in the past. You came because of what my father did. See? I'm attracting happiness with the luck my father saved, even now. Am I wrong about that?"

Masafumi looked at the driver's reflection in the mirror.

The driver smiled but didn't offer a response.

"The more I got to thinking, I realized I couldn't end my life so easily. If I did, I would have left this world only using the luck that the previous generation saved for us. Who knows how many years I have left, but I have to devote the rest of my life to saving luck for the next generation. When I looked at the soba, that's what I heard my father telling me."

"I see . . ." the driver murmured, bringing the taxi to a halt. "We're here. This is where you should be right now."

Masafumi looked out the window. There was a hardware store out front. It was a store he'd never seen before.

The meter now read 71,450. Though he'd only

been half listening, according to the driver's explanation, the taxi was all-you-can-ride until the meter ticked down to zero.

"Can I ask you a question?"

"Why, yes."

"You said that you would keep showing up until the meter hits zero."

"That's right."

"Okay. You also said the ride was already paid for. I didn't pay for it, and the payment probably isn't money. I'm not sure what it is, but someone must have done something to accumulate luck. Someone like my father. And it works something like this." Masafumi took out his shop's rewards card from his wallet and showed it to the driver. "There are points on this card because someone saved and never used them. I haven't saved any points, only used them. Am I wrong about that?"

The driver smiled.

"The remaining 71,450 yen on the meter there. I wonder if I can pass it on to someone else?"

"You mean you're not going to use it for yourself?"

"It's pitiful living off the luck that others have saved. Starting today, I'd like to live in a way that saves luck for the next generation."

"I understand. I'll be sure to save the remaining points for someone in the next generation to use someday."

"I'd be grateful if you do."

With that, Masafumi held out his hand, which the driver took in his and shook.

As soon as Masafumi reluctantly let go, the driver popped open the rear door.

Just as he was about to step out, Masafumi turned around as if remembering something. "Hey, one more thing. How do you accumulate luck anyway?"

It was the last question Masafumi asked the driver.

YES, BUT DEFINITELY NOT

The driver's story was so shocking that Shuichi was left speechless.

His paternal grandfather had been kind to him. He was always supportive and had a gentle smile, no matter what Shuichi did. That grandfather had died when Shuichi was in his first year of junior high school. His name was Kazunori. Although they were not biologically related, as far as Shuichi was concerned, that man was his grandfather.

His grandmother was the one who had told him about his biological grandfather who died in the war when his father was one year old. She had shown him a picture of him once. However, Shuichi had never given much thought to the man's existence, saying, "Okay, but I already have a grandfather."

Perhaps he was hesitant to acknowledge the existence of his biological grandfather out of consideration for the grandfather who was always kind to him. It was also the first time that he learned his biological grandfather's name was Ryozo.

Suddenly, the image of Ryozo, fully formed in shape and personality, floated into his head. What emerged was the smiling face of a man lit up in the glow of the Saipan sunset, who never attained anything he desired but instead sacrificed his life for the future happiness of children.

Considering this, Shuichi felt a pang of guilt, or perhaps it was a knot in his chest, for having lived his forty-five years without ever once thinking about Ryozo.

"Ryozo-san's life was hard from the moment he was born to his tragic end," continued the driver. "Some might chalk it up to the era. Nevertheless, all of Japan was engulfed in a turmoil that would be unimaginable to our generation. Despite that, Ryozo-san was always in good spirits. Though, as he witnessed the deaths of tens of thousands of his comrades on the battlefield, living every day on the brink of life and death, he couldn't maintain his spirits for long. Still, even on the night before his death, he was smiling. From today's perspective, he ended his short twenty-six years without having ever experienced good luck. But thanks to the luck that those of his generation accumulated, the next generation was able to bring about Japan's extraordinary postwar growth."

Listening to the driver with his arms folded across his chest, Shuichi responded with a contemplative groan. Though he'd imagined his grandfather as being much older, if he died at twenty-six, he had been much younger than Shuichi was now. It was a strange feeling.

"Now do you understand what I meant by 'yes, but definitely not'? There are people, like your grandfather, who sacrificed their lives for the sake of others while maintaining their spirits but died without ever having encountered an opportunity to change their luck. That's what was meant by 'yes.' But I also said 'definitely not' because the luck saved up by the previous generation is what enabled the next generation to thrive. That goes for you too. You grew up benefiting from the luck they saved up."

The driver paused his lengthy explanation and peered into Shuichi's face.

After a moment of silence, Shuichi said, "So you showed up in front of me because my father left what's on the fare meter for me. Is that it?"

"That's right." The driver nodded.

"And you're saying the luck my grandfather sacrificed his life accumulating was passed on to my father, who passed it on to me. You expect me to believe that?"

The driver shook his head. "You still don't quite

understand how the fruits of one's efforts become manifest. Okay, imagine this, if you will. Your daughter, Yumeka-san, will be taking her high school entrance exams next year. Right now, she doesn't go to school and spends all of her time at home with her smartphone like it's her only friend in the world. Let's say that a certain incident motivates her to go back to school and study again like she's completely transformed."

"What incident?"

"I don't know. It's just an example. Your daughter's transformation is dramatic enough to stun even you, as she spends nearly all her time studying. How do you think seeing her like that would make you feel? You would be pretty moved. Not only that, but you would also likely be motivated to work harder yourself."

"Yeah, I suppose."

"You go about your work as usual, but you can't seem to secure a contract. Just when you're thinking about calling it a day, the image of your daughter studying her heart out comes to mind. Inspired by your daughter, you decide to work a bit longer. And then, on the next visit, you secure a contract. In which case, your happiness can be said to have been the result of your daughter's efforts.

"In this way, your life begins to change a bit. But it isn't just you. Some of Yumeka-san's friends notice her transformation and start thinking that they need to get serious themselves. When their parents see them working hard, they in turn feel motivated to work harder, just as you did. You see, someone's earnest effort has the power to bring happiness to others."

Perhaps the driver was right. If Shuichi were witness to Yumeka's earnest efforts, that alone would give him a burst of energy.

"But what if," continued the driver. "Yumeka-san comes to believe effort is meaningless or that hard work doesn't necessarily lead to success?"

"Oh, come on . . ."

"It's possible. She's spent the better part of two years not studying. While it's all fine and good that an incident inspired her to study like crazy, none of it leads to good results. In time, she'll come to question whether there's any point in giving her best effort. And then, she begins to say, 'Effort isn't always rewarded.' What would you do if she started thinking that way?"

"I'd tell her that she's got it all wrong. I'd share with her how seeing her efforts inspired me and the good that happened as a result. Besides, it isn't that her efforts aren't being rewarded, it just takes a bit more time to see results, that's all. She can't give up until she achieves a breakthrough. Making up for those lost two years requires considerable effort."

The driver was smirking.

"What!" Shuichi said defensively.

"So, you do know."

"Know what?"

"That one's efforts will always be rewarded. Did you realize that Yumeka-san was you, and you were Masafumi-san in this story?"

"What do you mean?"

"I mean exactly that. When you were studying for

your entrance exams, your father must have watched you and thought many times about trying his best too. He experienced quite a bit of happiness as a result. Despite this, you believed that one's effort wouldn't always be rewarded. That's only natural, I suppose. After all, you ended up at your safety school rather than your top-choice university, which led to a breakup with your girlfriend at the time. So perhaps your belief that effort isn't always rewarded is expected. But if your father had known what you were thinking, I'm certain he would have told you exactly what you would have said to your daughter."

"What . . . ?"

"Your father had no idea you were thinking these things. If he had, he would have told you that thanks to your efforts, he was able to persevere. But don't blame your father. I mean, you never considered whether Yumeka-san was thinking that either."

"Well, I . . ." Shuichi was at a loss for words.

"In reality, the world is the collective energy derived from witnessing someone's efforts, not from the results achieved. Everyone accumulates energy, such as by seeing their daughter's perseverance, and becomes motivated to work harder themselves. It's this collective energy of working adults that drives society. I mean, you aren't drawing energy from the results that your daughter achieves, right?"

"Right . . ."

"Everyone in society draws energy by witnessing someone's efforts and uses it to motivate themselves. Yet when it comes to their efforts, they conclude, based on their narrow worldview and immediate outcomes, that they have bad luck or that their efforts are unrewarded. But people's efforts often come to fruition much later than expected. Sometimes ten years later, or in some cases, a hundred years."

"A hundred years . . ."

"That's right. Plus, those results may not necessarily manifest in the person who expended the effort. The results may manifest in a loved one or even in the next generation. Yet if something good doesn't happen to them immediately following their efforts or hard work, they make a big fuss. These people think too much of themselves and instant gratification. They fail to understand that their life is but one part of a continuous narrative of existence."

"A continuous narrative of existence?" Shuichi could only parrot back the driver's words.

"If you believe that your life ends with the completion of your story, then perhaps it's best to fulfill your desires using the conditions given to you at birth. But in reality, life is only a part of an eternal narrative of existence. Your life was also inherited from Ryozo-san and Masafumi-san and is being passed on to Yumeka-san.

"But what's being passed on isn't just your life. You were born and raised in a society created by someone other than yourself. It was created by people like Ryozo-san and Masafumi-san.

"If you believe yourself to have been born when times were good, you might think you were lucky, but you didn't just happen to be born and raised in a lucky, peaceful, and prosperous era that came out of thin air. It's something that was born from blood, sweat, tears, effort, and in extreme cases, lives.

"Each person does their best to contribute their part to the eternal narrative of existence, so the next generation can be born and raised in a better era than the generation before. And now, you have taken the baton to live out your part of the eternal narrative."

Shuichi looked back on his life up to now.

Every one of the driver's words struck a chord with him.

He'd been told, "You were born in a good era," since childhood by his parents and his teachers. All of the adults in his life had told him so. It was no wonder. Those adults had all experienced war. To the generation that had lived through the war as children or as parents of children, the period of prosperity from 1975 must have felt like a dream.

But to Shuichi, that life was nothing more than what was *there*.

Urged to pursue and realize their dreams during what was known as the peaceful age or the plentiful age, Shuichi's was the first generation where everyone was expected to go to college. Having to endure university entrance examinations with 10 percent admission rates, they came to harbor resentment toward the so-called exam wars.

They cursed the era, questioning why they had to study so much.

After hearing about his grandfather's experience in Saipan from the driver, however, Shuichi felt that it was wrong to compare his admissions struggle to war, and his face flushed with shame.

As the era shifted to the '90s, children were no longer told that they were experiencing a fortunate time, and Shuichi had never personally experienced anything resembling prosperity. Despite chipping away at his slice of happiness daily, he had reached his present age without ever having attained any stability or peace of mind. The current generation who was of child-rearing age, including himself, began to feel sorry for today's children. It was astonishing how much had changed in a mere forty years.

THE LUCKY RIDE

THE DRIVER'S WORDS HAD GIVEN SHUICHI PAUSE.

Even at this very moment, newborns were coming into the world, knowing nothing about present society. Just who had created this society?

It was us.

Shuichi was certain of it.

Until then, Shuichi had never considered that he had helped create society as it was now. He had assumed that the world was the way it was due to some influential political figure or pressure from abroad, and had never once questioned it. That was why he had no qualms about criticizing society. Realizing now that he had a part in creating that very environment, however, he was hard-pressed to criticize it. He felt sorry for the newborns being born at this moment.

Why did he feel this way now? He couldn't quite say. Perhaps he never felt this way before because he knew nothing about the past.

From the moment he had come into the world, his life goal was set. It was to acquire as much as possible and to be as happy as possible. He was taught that was the very definition of happiness and never questioned it. However, if his generation was only a tiny part of the eternal life narrative to acquire anything and that happiness was achieved only by using all the luck accumulated by previous generations, could he celebrate that achievement fully? Should he even want that kind of happiness?

Once he collected his thoughts, Shuichi let out a deep sigh.

"Maybe I've been wrong all along," he murmured. "I grew up in an era where we believed those who acquire more than others are successful and those who don't acquire anything are failures. So, being successful has always been my life goal since I was a kid, which basically meant that I had to acquire more than anyone else. I thought that was what was expected, so I never doubted it for even a minute. But maybe we shouldn't be chasing that kind of happiness.

"Considering we're only living a tiny part of the eternal narrative of existence, if we choose to live that way, believing that we have a right to use up all the luck that our ancestors saved and the luck we saved ourselves, then there would be nothing left. If that happens, then people will come to say that the next generation was unfortunate to be born in such an era. Is that it?"

"Well, I'm not so sure," replied the driver.

Shuichi, expecting the driver to agree with him, was surprised by his uncertainty.

"You mean that's not it?"

"Perhaps we could do with . . . what was it again? It was a term a passenger I gave a ride to had used a while back, fifteen years ago. Ah, that's right. A positive mindset! We could do with a positive mindset."

"A positive mindset?" Shuichi's voice cracked. "That's not likely," he said with a restrained chuckle.

"Why do you say that?"

"It's not something I'm good at."

Shuichi was aware that having a positive mindset was good. At least, he thought it was. And yet he couldn't help that he held a negative outlook on things.

He tried to be positive but just couldn't bring himself to think that way. He was negative to the core. When he thought about what might happen next, he tended to spend more time dwelling on things getting worse rather than better.

He would start to think, *Things never go your way so easily*, then *What if this happens or that happens*, and before long, his thoughts would plunge into negativity until he lost the will to act.

Despite this, his sales job frequently required him to make office visits, most of which ended in disappointment and usually confirmed his belief that things wouldn't work out as he hoped.

Positive thinkers might argue that things turned out badly because he wasn't approaching opportunities with a positive mindset. As he accumulated experiences of going into sales meetings with a positive attitude only to see them end in disappointment, he found it increasingly difficult to feel that way.

"I've had things not going the way I hoped for over forty years. Suddenly, someone tells me that positivity is important, and I'm supposed to believe that if I focus on the positive, things will start to go my way. Even if that were true, it's not for me. Sorry, but it's just not the way I'm wired."

"Well, of course not! That's not what positive thinking is at all."

"What?" Shuichi blurted out.

"Think about it. No one can tell whether something is positive or negative while that something is happening. Life is about changing whatever happens into a necessary experience in your life. In that sense, something can turn into a positive experience, or conversely, a negative one. Imagining something going your way and it actually happening isn't positive thinking. True positive thinking is about seeing everything that happens in life as necessary no matter what it is. It's not about thinking positively toward what might happen but toward what did happen."

The mass cancellation of contracts from several days ago came to Shuichi's mind.

Could he truly accept that incident as a necessary

experience in his life? Shuichi shook his head. There was no way he could see it as a positive. After suffering such a painful experience, how could he possibly accept it as a good thing?

"I don't think this positive thinking stuff is for me."

The driver smiled. "Of course, we're bound to encounter failures, unexpected misfortunes, and sudden natural disasters in our lifetime that we can't accept as positive the instant they happen. It's natural not to think so right away. Eventually, though, there may come a day when we can. What I meant earlier is: What if we tried to understand positive thinking a bit differently?"

"Differently?"

"Do you remember what I said about how our lives are but a part of a continuous narrative of existence?"

"Yeah."

"So, when you enter this continuous narrative—that is when you are born into the world—you inherit the benefits of the story that came before you, right?"

"Okay."

"You're born into this narrative, live for about a hundred years, and then you die. At that moment of your death, you leave behind more benefits than when you entered the story, making the narrative a little more positive through your existence. That's what true positive thinking is about."

"You save more luck than you use."

"Exactly. That amounts to a positive, right? It's the role of those of us living in the present as part of an ongoing narrative."

"My role."

"Okada-san, you mentioned earlier that 'we shouldn't be chasing that kind of happiness.' But there's no need to hold back. It's perfectly fine to want things. As long as you live in a way where you accumulate more luck than you use, you can say you're fulfilling your role, and that's still a net positive."

"Maybe you're right . . ."

"It's about living in a way where you save more luck than you use. About using half of the accumulated luck and still having more to gain than anyone else. That's how one lives with a truly positive mindset. That's my belief."

Suddenly, the calligraphy framed in Wakiya's office flashed across Shuichi's mind like a neon sign.

"Stay positive, and laugh more than anyone else!" he exclaimed.

"Yes, that's the way! Be a person whom everyone thinks has it better than anyone else. But for that person, the luck they've used is only a small part of the luck they saved. Don't you think that's an incredible way to live?"

Suddenly, the world seemed to brighten before his eyes. Shuichi felt goosebumps spread over his entire body.

The driver's perspective was a departure from the concept of positive thinking that Shuichi had in his mind. If the driver was saying that living a life that saved more luck for the next generation than the luck that you used was positive thinking, it was a perspective Shuichi could easily accept as his own. It was the kind of life he wanted to lead.

That value system was different from what was considered "normal" nowadays. It felt like being told to strive to lose rather than gain in life. He was being told to do more for others and minimize personal gain, producing a net positive in the process. That was the kind of life he was being urged to lead.

Those words captivated him and didn't let go. He felt the deepest part of his heart longing for exactly that. It wasn't reason but emotion—or, better yet, his soul—that was urging him to aspire to such a life. The goosebumps were evidence of that.

"The truth is I never liked the phrase, 'positive mindset.' But that was because I didn't correctly understand its true meaning," said Shuichi thoughtfully.

"I'm not sure if that's the true meaning or not. The meaning can vary from person to person."

"Maybe you're right."

Shuichi checked the meter, realizing he'd been in the taxi for longer than usual. It read 39,330. He looked out the window to find a neighborhood he knew well.

At that moment, he understood where his final destination would be.

This is it.

He reached this decision while listening to the driver's story.

The driver, perhaps anticipating this since the discussion about Masafumi, drove in silence as though he were cherishing his last moments with Shuichi.

THE LAST LESSON

"Hey?" Shuichi said to the driver while gazing out the window. "We're almost to the destination, aren't we?"

The driver smiled. "I guess it's pretty obvious."

"Yeah. Which brings me to a favor I'd like to ask."

"I had an inkling, but I suppose I should ask what it is anyway."

Despite the driver's somewhat irritating manner of

speaking, Shuichi couldn't help but smile. "I figured you would, and you'd be right. You don't have to come anymore. Instead, I'd like you to use what's left on the meter for—"

He started to say *for my daughter* but swallowed his words. That was wishful thinking. It was up to the driver to decide who to pick up.

"—the next generation."

The driver nodded once. "I understand. Well then, it's almost time to say goodbye," he said, stopping the meter.

"Hey, are you sure you want to do that?"

"Yes, the rest of the way is on me."

"Oh, well, thanks. Maybe you can answer one last question. If I'm honest, I have no confidence at all."

Shuichi's voice softened. He spoke as if he were a child seeking an answer from Ryozo or Masafumi, rather than talking to the young driver.

"I've never won anything in competition. Compared to others, I don't have any notable talents. Despite my best efforts, I've never been praised for anything since I was a kid, but that doesn't mean I have the grit to work harder than anyone else either. As embarrassed as I am to admit this at my age, I don't think I'm cut out for my current job. My sales performance hasn't improved and the contracts that I busted my butt to secure ended up getting canceled. At this rate, there's no way that I can continue. Then again, I can't exactly think of any other job that I'm suited for. Even though, as a father, I'm always on my daughter's case about studying, I don't have confidence in my parenting skills.

"When I look at Yumeka, who's stopped going to school, I can't help but wonder if everything I've done is wrong. I'm barely keeping it together at work, and despite knowing something's got to give, I've lost confidence and feel as if I'm on the verge of a breakdown. Do you still believe there's a role for someone like me to play?"

It was a candid admission of his feelings. Surely, he wouldn't have been able to admit such things to anyone else. The only reason he could now was because it was the driver whom he was confiding in. It was upon deciding never to see the driver again that he knew he had to ask.

The driver flashed a broad smile and answered immediately, "Of course there is. An important role only you can fulfill. You've been fulfilling that role up until now and will continue to do so in the future."

"If you say so, then it must be true. But I just don't have the confidence in myself. What should I do?"

"The first thing is to stop comparing yourself to others. Stop comparing your life to the lives of others and focus on your own. All the others are going about their lives, fulfilling their roles. It doesn't matter that they have a lot, or that things are going well for them. Instead, take a good look at your own life. Then, you'll realize how blessed you are. Start by genuinely acknowledging the blessings in your life. It all starts there. If you can see that with your whole heart, you'll start to believe that there isn't anyone more blessed than yourself."

"Acknowledge the blessings in my life . . . I understand everything you said intellectually but with my whole heart? That's easier said than done."

"Completely understandable, given your catastrophe at your job."

"You sure know how to rub it in."

The driver gave him an impish smile. "Say, what did you eat for breakfast this morning?"

"Why are you asking? What does that have to do with anything?"

"Humor me, please. What did you have?"

"This morning? Just the standard miso soup and rice. And natto beans. Oh, and some sausage and eggs."

"Would you believe me if I told you that it takes the entire universe to prepare that meal—no, to prepare even the bowl of rice you had this morning?"

"The entire universe?"

"That's right. Sounds spectacular, I know, but it's true. How is rice produced, for example?"

"It's planted and grown in fields."

"Right. Rice can't be made unless there's a field

and people to grow it. Even with people, if there are no machines, rice can't be made available in such abundance. That's why tractors are necessary. But they wouldn't be made without people to develop the tech, make the molds, and manufacture them. Not only that, the materials, such as iron, copper, and aluminum needed to manufacture the tractors, as well as the quartz needed to make glass, are all imported from places like China, Australia, and Africa. Which means people are necessary to mine and transport these materials to Japan.

"Then we need ships, and that's where shipbuilders come in. Transportation companies too. Tractors, ships, and the machinery used for excavating all operate on diesel. That diesel is mined from the US and countries in the Middle East. The people in those industries are needed. In the first place, diesel and gasoline are fossil fuels, meaning they come from prehistoric organisms. This means that for billions of years, since the emergence of life on Earth, there has existed a continuous chain of life.

"I can go on and on and raise more examples of the things and people that are indispensable in producing a single bowl of rice, but for the sake of time, I'll stop there.

"Despite having all of these components, we still can't simply produce rice. We rely on the sun. Now, this is where the rest of the universe comes into play. With the sun alone, plants will wither and die. That's because they require water. If you give them ample water and sunlight, will rice be made? Something's still missing: carbon dioxide.

"Because carbon dioxide is produced through animal respiration, rice plants wouldn't grow without our breathing. Since rice is produced by the energy of the sun, water, and carbon dioxide, its basic ingredients are carbon dioxide, hydrogen, and oxygen. Humans consume the rice, converting it into energy to live. This means that these ingredients constitute humans and are also the parts that keep us functioning. Do you know their origins?"

"That would be . . ."

Shuichi found himself unable to respond. The driver's story was so spectacular in scope that, though Shuichi comprehended the words, he struggled to keep up. Like a student who was unexpectedly called on in class, he panicked.

"Something from Earth?"

"Things that we find on Earth weren't always there to begin with. Where did they originate? They were formed from the particles of stars, like the sun, during supernova explosions that occur at the end of stars' lives, scattering throughout space. In essence, we all originated from stars."

The driver took a breath to compose himself, realizing he'd been speaking rapidly.

"Even for a single bowl of rice, the entire universe is indispensable, as are the activities of every human on Earth. If you understand that, perhaps you'd think of yourself as fortunate to have had that meal today. We consume such meals every day as a matter of routine, but for those who can't see their lives as being blessed, just what kind of life would bring them that sense of being truly fortunate? Perhaps it's impossible for them to feel that way no matter what they have."

The taxi turned at the final corner. In two hundred meters, they would arrive at the doorstep of Shuichi's childhood home.

"I hope you'll consider the rest on your own. In time, you'll come to feel like there's no one more blessed than you. Once you reach that point, you'll gain confidence in yourself and wholeheartedly believe that you have a role to fulfill."

The driver brought the taxi to a halt, popped open the rear door, and turned around to regard him. Shuichi said nothing, staring at the driver's face. He wanted to speak but struggled to find the right words. How long had they been like this? In the end, Shuichi nodded a few times to reassure himself, then put on a smile.

"Listen, I'm sorry that I've been rude to you."

The driver shook his head. "It's all right."

Shuichi extended his hand. "Thank you. You're not

so much a taxi driver as a luck changer who turned my life around."

"Luck changer? Hmm, I rather like the sound of that. Maybe I should start calling myself that."

The driver shook Shuichi's hand and returned a smile.

"Oh, hey!" Suddenly remembering something, the driver rummaged around the passenger seat and held out a tiny paper bag. "Here, take this."

"What is it?"

Shuichi took the bag and opened it on the spot. Inside was a black bass figurine about five centimeters long with its mouth wide open, its body curled into a U shape. A fishing hook was stuck in its mouth with a string representing a fishing line at the end. It looked like a black bass that had been freshly caught.

"It's a cellphone charm. A memento of your ride. I hope you'll make use of it."

Shuichi burst into a chuckle. "I would've expected a tiny taxi or something. But a black bass? I don't even fish."

The driver was grinning. "Please, I insist."

Shuichi smiled back. "Okay, I accept. Take an interest in everything, right?"

With that, he quickly got out of the taxi.

When he turned around, the driver closed the rear door immediately, seemingly without any wistfulness about parting. As the taxi pulled away, the driver raised his hand in what seemed like a gesture of farewell. Although his face was hidden from view, preventing confirmation, the way he raised his head was eerily similar to that of Shuichi's father, Masafumi.

"Dad . . . ?"

By the time the thought entered Shuichi's mind, the taxi had already driven off and he couldn't see the face of the man behind the wheel.

As Shuichi watched the taxi go, the time he'd spent in the vehicle only moments ago seemed to him like a dream. As if to confirm that it had indeed happened, he stared at the black bass figurine in his hand and clenched it tightly.

After tucking the charm in his pocket, Shuichi walked up to the entrance and rang the intercom.

"Coming!"

It was the familiar voice of his mother, Tamiko.

She would be surprised to see him. Shuichi hadn't planned to come, so it wasn't until that moment that he ran his head in overdrive for an excuse for why he had come.

A SECOND CHANCE AT LIFE

As soon as Tamiko recognized it was Shuichi at the door, the first words out of her mouth were predictable:

"Would it have killed you to let me know you were coming?"

Though she seemed to imply that his unannounced visit was an imposition, her expression appeared glad. That was to be expected. It had only been six months since she started living on her own. She likely wasn't used to being alone and was feeling lonely.

"Sorry, Mom."

"Did you eat?"

"Not yet."

It was typical of his mother to worry about his stomach. Hearing this made him instantly feel like he was home.

"I didn't know you were coming, so I don't have anything made. Can you wait while I whip something up?"

"Sure. I'm not in any hurry."

"What brings you by?"

Tamiko's back as she was going down the hall looked quite a bit smaller than he remembered.

"I happened to be out this way for work. I was planning to go straight home, then I remembered there was something you wanted to discuss."

She went into the kitchen and opened the refrigerator. Perhaps she intended to talk about whatever it was later.

Rather than sitting at the table next to the kitchen, Shuichi went into the adjacent living room and sat on the sofa. The couch had lost most of its spring and caved in when he sat on it. The view from that seat had hardly changed in over twenty years.

When he looked toward the kitchen, Tamiko was putting the frying pan on the stove. He'd always pictured his mother efficiently going about her housework, but the woman before him was clumsy and slow, as if he were watching a slow-motion video. She was growing old.

"You want me to do it?" he called out.

"It's okay. I'm used to it. You sit there," she answered cheerfully.

As he looked about the room to get a sense of his mother's daily routine, he got up from the sofa, suddenly remembering something.

"Say, Mom? Do you remember that time about twenty-five years ago when I was in college and Dad suddenly said he was going hiking one morning?"

Tamiko stopped what she was doing and turned to

Shuichi with a look of surprise. "Why, yes. How do you know that?"

"It's not important. Anyway, did he happen to buy something strange that day?"

Looking down at her hands working the knife, she smiled. "He sure did."

"What was it?"

"It's in the bedroom on your father's dresser."

Shuichi headed into his parents' bedroom. The room, about the size of six tatami mats, contained only two dressers and a new bed that his mother slept in, but the furniture's enormous size took up nearly the entire room. His mother and father used to sleep on traditional Japanese futons, but now that she was alone, his mother had switched to a bed, complaining of the daily burden of laying out and putting away the futon.

Shuichi looked on top of the double-door dresser. There was a large bundle wrapped in a purple cloth protruding from the edge. Shuichi reached his full height and carefully brought it down. There seemed to be several tools placed on top of a wooden board large enough to hold with both hands. He carried it to the kitchen and set it down on the table.

"I just cleaned it yesterday. I didn't want it to grow mold from neglect," she said.

Shuichi noticed there wasn't a speck of dust on the cloth. Carefully, he untied the knot.

"Well, I'll be . . ." Shuichi muttered to himself.

Inside were tools for making soba noodles. Every one of the tools had seen considerable use over the years.

"One day out of the blue, your father left the house, saying he was going for a hike for the first time in twenty years. But he came back almost immediately with an exact set of tools like this one."

His father must have bought the set of tools, replacing them time and again as they wore down from use.

"Dad? Making soba? I can't picture it."

"Oh? He got rather good at it. From that day on, he practiced making soba just about every day, to the point that when I think of your father, I think of soba."

"I didn't know he picked up another hobby after golf."

"I don't know what possessed him to suddenly start making soba, but he was quite passionate about it."

Tamiko's ignorance about the truth seemed to indicate that his father had not told her about Ryozo. Because of what the driver had told him, Shuichi understood keenly why his father had wanted to learn to make soba. No doubt he wanted to make the delicious noodles that his father had so craved for him. Though Ryozo's dream of eating them again never came to pass, Masafumi wanted at least to be able to report back once he'd learned to make the noodles. That must have been foremost on his mind.

"When sales at the shop started to go down, and a while after he quit golfing, I thought he found a new hobby too. But that wasn't the case."

"What do you mean?"

"I mean that this wasn't just a hobby. Your father really was trying to become a soba master."

"A master?"

"Yes, your father realized that the novelty shop wasn't ever going to right itself, so he decided he was going to start a soba shop."

"A soba shop?"

"Not just any ordinary soba shop, but a truly spectacular one. It was always my job to taste the soba he made. Every time that I did, he would ask, 'Well, is it the best soba in Japan?' Then, I'd tell him, 'I don't know if it's the best, but it is delicious.' But he insisted that it had to be the best in Japan. He said that truly delicious soba shops could be in the mountains or someplace remote, and people would still come from all over the country."

"The best soba shop in Japan . . ."

Tamiko smiled fondly. "But you know, I'm not just saying this. Your father's soba truly was delicious. At first, it was too soft or too tough, or sometimes, it lacked chewiness and was too crumbly. Every batch tasted different. But over time, it became more consistent with every batch, and around the fifth year, it might have been better than some well-known soba shops. By the tenth year, I couldn't find soba anywhere that tasted better than your father's. It just might have been the best in Japan."

"Hang on, Dad practiced for ten years?"

"It wasn't just ten years. He kept at it until he died, so that would make it twenty-five years."

Shuichi was stunned. Stunned that his father had been so dedicated to soba making, but the biggest shock was that he hadn't known what his father had been up to for twenty-five years.

"If he learned to make such good soba, why didn't he try to open a shop?"

"About ten years into it, your father became confident that his soba truly could compete with the best of them. He looked for properties, requested loans from banks, and got to work in other ways, but it never panned out. The timing was awful. It was around the time he closed the novelty shop, and we were bleeding money just by keeping it open. At that time, your father was already sixty, and given his age, none of the banks would lend him the seed money to start the shop. He was furious that the banks refused 'without even tasting his soba.'"

"I had no idea," murmured Shuichi.

"I suggested that he ask you to go into business together. Most banks were willing to approve a loan if the son was involved. But then . . ."

"Then?" Shuichi leaned forward in anticipation.

"He said that your life was yours to live. He didn't want to involve you in his selfish dream, so he told me to keep it to myself. This was when you had just gotten married and he didn't want to trouble you. In the end, your father had no choice but to give up on taking out a loan. But you know what? He never stopped making soba."

"Even after he'd given up on opening a shop?"

"It was so if you ever came home to tell him that you were ready to start a business, he could offer to help if it was a soba shop. Unlike him, you graduated college. Not only that, you graduated with a business degree and have been in sales for years, so you could be an owner. Since those were things he wasn't good at, I guess he wanted to be of use as an artisan."

"I'll be damned." Shuichi was speechless.

"He wasn't honest with you, I know. He didn't want to hold you back, because he loved you. And his wanting to be there to support you if you ever got into trouble? That's love too. So when he realized he couldn't have the shop, he didn't seem all that disappointed. He went right on perfecting his soba-making skills like before."

It was likely that his father persevered knowing that he was accumulating luck.

"Toward the end, his feelings seemed to have changed a bit," continued Tamiko. "You became busy after you switched jobs and began selling insurance. You stopped coming home to visit, and the few times we talked on the phone, you sounded rushed, irritated, and your father must have sensed something, sensed that you might be at a dead end in life. That's why he started saying that he wanted to make you his soba noodles."

"So that's why." Shuichi recalled every time they

talked on the phone, his father had always asked him when he was coming for a visit in his later years. It wasn't like his father to ask such a question, so he imagined that his father was getting sentimental with age, but it was the opposite. He had seen his son's sorry state and had reached out to try to help him in any way he could.

Shuichi gazed at the well-worn tools. He felt a warm sting in the recesses of his nose. Masafumi was able to taste the soba noodles that his father, Ryozo, so wanted him to have. From there, he had embarked on a new life. Shuichi, however, had let his father die without having ever tasted his soba. He felt as if he had committed the greatest betrayal that a son could make against his father.

"In the end, all of his efforts didn't pay off," Tamiko remarked.

Hearing this, Shuichi shook his head. "There's no such thing as effort that doesn't pay off, Mom."

Tamiko's eyes widened as she peered into his face. "That was what your father said too."

"Well, he's right." Shuichi nodded repeatedly to

himself in satisfaction. Struggling to hold back the tears, he said, "Say, Mom. Would you mind if I took these tools with me?"

Tamiko nodded with a smile. "Of course. It was nice having them. It was as if your father was still here, but I think he would be happier if you kept them."

Shuichi wrapped the set of soba-making tools back in the purple cloth and took it off the table.

"I'll put it in the other room for now."

As soon as he turned his back to Tamiko, tears rolled down his face. As he went down the hall, it felt as though Masafumi might emerge from the sliding door on the other end at any moment. Shuichi murmured, *I'm sorry, Dad*, again and again in his heart.

With every murmur, his eyes pooled with tears.

Tamiko was alone, crying in the kitchen.

SHUICHI LEFT EARLY THE NEXT MORNING.

At dinner the night before, he had asked, "By the way, what did you want to talk to me about?" to which his mother chuckled and answered, "I already told you."

When Shuichi visited, she had planned to tell him the story about his father's soba.

"I didn't expect you to know your father had brought something on his way back from hiking. You really surprised me," Tamiko said repeatedly.

When Shuichi transferred trains in Nagoya, it was already 8:30 a.m. He called Wakiya, told him his whereabouts and that he would be late to the office, and then got on the bullet train.

Wakiya had said nothing apart from hinting to bring back a souvenir or two. Since Shuichi had made the call after going through the ticket gate, he ran into a gift shop inside the waiting room. He thought about what to buy, but as soon as he reached the aisles, he knew exactly what to purchase.

The bullet train was nearly full, and although he had managed to get a middle seat, the child being held by the woman in the window seat had spilled a drink, and Shuichi was unable to sit in the wet seat.

"Sorry, I'll move so you can sit here," the woman said, making to get up with the child in her arms, but Shuichi raised a hand for her to stay.

"That's all right. You stay there. I'll ask the conductor onboard to find me another seat," Shuichi said and exited the car.

He found the conductor somewhere around car no. 8, explained the situation, and was escorted to the first-class Green Car.

"All of our regular-class seats are fully booked, so please take this seat."

Shuichi let slip a tiny smile, wondering whether he might have used some of his luck by being gifted an upgraded seat. In that instant, he realized he had internalized the driver's teachings.

He excused himself to the businessman working on his laptop in the adjacent seat and sat down.

"INSURANCE IS A PRODUCT THAT EMBODIES THE spirit of mutual assistance. It's a gathering of people who support each other in times of need."

"Fascinating. That's exactly the kind of company I'd like to create."

"Let's say, for example, a hundred people decided to pool their money every month. Everyone has the right to use that money when they're struggling. But since 'struggling' has different standards for different people, there are agreements in place to determine when money can be used. That's why when you hear the term 'whole life insurance,' it feels like you're losing when nothing happens to you. But insurance isn't about buying peace of mind the way people will have you think. Insurance isn't so much about saving up for your future self but about helping someone who's struggling now. And because you're also paying into the pool, you're also entitled to receive help when you need it. Anyway, that's the way I see it."

Shuichi was giving an earnest explanation about life insurance to Yamamoto, who was sitting next to him.

Encounters were indeed unpredictable. Yamamoto was the owner of eight restaurants in and around Nagoya. He was on his way to a business seminar in Yokohama when Shuichi sat down next to him.

Of course, that alone wouldn't necessarily lead to a conversation about insurance. About the time the bullet train passed Hamamatsu, Yamamoto began to fidget, and thinking he wanted to go to the bathroom, Shuichi had asked, "Would you like me to let you by?"

Shaking his head, the man asked, "Where did you get that?" pointing to the black bass figurine dangling from Shuichi's bag. Yamamoto said it was a rare item, legendary among collectors.

Shuichi offered casually, "You're welcome to have it," removed the figurine from his bag, and held it out toward him.

The charm wasn't anything he had an interest in any way. The driver had likely given it to him to create a luck-changing opportunity.

That was how the conversation started.

When Shuichi mentioned that he sold life insurance, Yamamoto, seeming to take an interest, asked, "Tell me more."

His restaurants were doing well and turning a profit.

The conversation started with the idea of buying insurance as a tax shelter.

Rather than explain the specific products that his company offered, Shuichi spoke more generally about what insurance was.

"I see," said Yamamoto, nodding. "So, with whole life insurance, you're not just buying peace of mind. By contributing to the pool, you're helping fellow insurance members who are in need."

"That's right."

"You make a compelling case. I imagine that's how salesmen like you turn a profit too."

Shuichi grinned and nodded. "Sure, insurance salesmen also benefit from this mutual assistance. We receive a percentage of the premiums for the first year, which is how we earn a living, so we're also dependent on this system of mutual assistance. But only for the first year. From the second year on, we hardly receive anything."

"Is that right?"

"It is. So, if you're thinking about buying insurance, you should find someone you can trust enough to want them to benefit from the sale and consult with them thoroughly until you're satisfied before making a purchase."

"Wait, I can't buy it from you, Okada-san?"

"Who, me?"

"Yeah, I've chatted with a few insurance salesmen before, but you're the first to tell me that buying whole life insurance isn't just about buying peace of mind. You're the one I trust."

Shuichi grimaced.

"I'm afraid I'm not cut out for this job. I'm thinking of a career change."

"Really?"

Shuichi nodded.

"But how am I going to repay you for the cell phone charm?"

Shuichi chuckled. "You were going to buy life insurance for a toy? That's going too far, Yamamoto-san. As I said, you should take some time to think things over carefully."

"I was going to purchase insurance anyway. But

if I'm going to do it, I'd like to do it with you," said Yamamoto, scratching his head.

"If you're serious about buying insurance, I'd be happy to introduce you to someone I trust. I'd be grateful if you'd speak to him."

"And you're all right with that, Okada-san?"

"Yes, but please take some time to consider whether you truly want to join. And if you do decide to join, don't cancel it right away. Think of yourself as becoming a part of a team that helps others."

Saying this, Shuichi exchanged business cards with Yamamoto.

"So, have you already decided what you're going to do?" asked Yamamoto.

Shuichi cracked an uneasy smile. "I don't know whether I'll amount to anything, but I'd like to be a soba master one day." He pointed to the purple-colored bundle on the rack overhead.

"Oh, have you been practicing as a hobby or something?"

"No, but soon."

Yamamoto's face froze in shock. It seemed people utterly lost the power of speech when they were shocked. However, it was Shuichi himself who was most surprised by the words. It was an inadvertent declaration that he wanted to become a soba master. He didn't understand why he'd blurted out such a thing. That those words came naturally was evidence of his deep desire for it.

Yamamoto got off the bullet train at Shin-Yokohama.

Shuichi gazed idly at the Tokyo skyline from the window. It had truly been a strange few days. It would take some time to recall everything that happened to him. However, there was no doubt that the last several days were a turning point in his life. He tried to remember the driver's face, but he couldn't recall it with any clarity. In retrospect, the man's face seemed to resemble that of his father in his younger days or that of someone else entirely. He had ridden in a mysterious taxi and conversed with the driver while being taken to various places. Now that he'd given away the only proof of those events, he couldn't confidently say that it had happened at all.

The only evidence to indicate it wasn't all a dream was Yamamoto's business card, which he had received in exchange.

That was how things gradually became part of the past.

A FRESH START

Shuichi returned to the office around eleven o'clock. Although Wakiya didn't appear to be particularly angry, he was waiting for Shuichi to report in. Shuichi walked up to Wakiya's desk. Strangely, he wasn't nervous.

"I'm sorry I'm late. I brought you a little something."

He offered Wakiya a box of Akafuku. While it was

a delicacy of Ise, it was a popular gift that was also sold at Nagoya Station.

"Hey, Akafuku! I couldn't get enough of these mochi treats when I was a kid."

He gladly accepted the gift, but as soon as he set it aside on the desk, he stared expectantly at Shuichi.

"So?"

He was demanding an explanation for why he'd been in Nagoya.

"Given how I lost those contracts at Saido Seminars this month, I had to secure a new contract, so I made a few visits to some contacts from the family business."

"Where was your family home again?"

"Gifu."

"Ah, that's right."

"A Yamamoto-san, who owns eight restaurants in Nagoya, had an interest in insurance, so I met with him and discussed it."

"Did you get the contract?"

"He's interested and likely to join, but I wasn't

able to earn enough of his trust to close the deal. He asked to meet with someone else to discuss it further, so I gave him your name and told him the company president himself would reach out at a later date."

Wakiya stared at Shuichi's expression for a while, then eventually said, "All right," extending a hand.

Shuichi handed him Yamamoto's business card, which he'd received on the bullet train and excused himself.

UPON SEEING SHUICHI RETURN HOME, YUKO WAS surprised.

"What's that?" she asked.

"This? I'll explain later."

"Is this . . . a soba-making set?" Taking the purple bundle from him, she eyed it closely.

"Yeah," Shuichi answered, taking off his shoes and hurrying into the bedroom.

He seemed more cheerful in Yuko's eyes.

Her prediction that something good had happened

was proven false when he explained after dinner. As soon as dinner was finished, Yumeka retreated into her room as usual. After the table was cleared and Yuko washed the dishes, Shuichi retrieved the bundle from the bedroom, set it down on the dining table, and untied the knot to reveal its contents.

"Okay, we established that you brought home a soba-making set, but why? They don't exactly look new."

Shuichi nodded. "It's kind of a keepsake of my dad."

"It's your dad's? I didn't know he made soba as a hobby."

Impressed, Yuko picked up the tools and studied them. She noticed that each tool had been well used over the years.

"Before we get into that, there's something I need to apologize about."

"About what?"

Yuko furrowed her brows and braced herself. She set the tools back down on the table, drew out a chair, and sat down.

"About a week ago, I had some contracts canceled. Twenty contracts, to be exact."

As soon as she heard the number, she realized it was the teachers working at the cram school that Shuichi had signed up ten months ago.

It felt just like yesterday when they were celebrating over it.

"I tried everything I could this week to recover the contracts, but I struck out. The next payday is going to be about half of what it's been."

She didn't ask how they were going to make ends meet. Instead, she responded, "Well, what happened, happened. Besides, another two months would have made a full year, and you would have experienced a salary cut anyway."

Perhaps it was because, somewhere deep down, she knew that this was always a possibility as long as Shuichi was in this line of work but also because she assumed he would've done something if he could. Shuichi was surprised at how calm Yuko was.

He was prepared for her to yell about why he had

kept silent about it for so long. At the very least, he expected her to heave a sigh or two with an icy expression and mutter, "This is a nightmare . . ." under her breath.

Was it that she didn't fully comprehend the gravity of the situation? Summoning every ounce of courage, he decided to tell her everything.

"I appreciate you saying so, but if a contract is canceled within a year, the amount of the premiums received so far must be refunded. Most likely, they'll deduct what they can from my next bonus and future bonuses, which means there won't be a bonus for quite some time. We're going to have to give up on the summer vacation we had planned. At this rate, we may also have to dip into Yumeka's education fund to get by. I'll talk with Yumeka and let her know that she may not be able to go to her choice of high school like we told her."

Yuko nodded repeatedly as if to convince herself. Upon seeing her reaction, Shuichi bowed his head deeply.

"I'm sorry."

Yuko put on a smile. "I don't know, maybe this was for the best."

"What?" Shuichi looked at Yuko in shock.

The Yuko he knew would have gotten upset and strung together complaints like "How did this happen!" and "You have to tell me these things sooner. I have plans too, you know!" But she didn't react this way at all.

"Did you say 'for the best'?" he asked a bit nervously.

"Yeah, who knows what will happen, but maybe this is an opportunity for Yumeka to think about her future. Maybe this is a sign that we shouldn't go on the trip. I'm sure we'll look back on this someday and see it as a blessing in disguise."

"I'm grateful that you'd say that. But there is one more thing I have to tell you."

"What is it?"

"I'm thinking of quitting my job. This whole incident has taught me that I'm not cut out for it."

"Then this is . . ." Yuko stared at the soba-making tools spread out on the table.

Shuichi shook his head. "I have a dream of opening a soba shop one day. But to realize that dream, I have to learn how to make the best soba in Japan. Since I haven't tried making soba yet, you might think that I'm full of it, but I'm committed to practicing for as long as it takes. And only when you think that it's the best soba in Japan will I even consider opening a shop."

"Me?"

"Yes, you. I won't open the shop until you say it's good enough."

Yuko laughed. "What are you going to do until then?"

"Nothing's set in stone yet, but I intend to find a soba shop where I can work during the day, and a good-paying job at night."

"Are you sure? I'm concerned about how you'll hold up."

Shuichi smiled. "I'll be fine. I have a life goal now."

For the first time, he realized that he had a clear goal to pursue. The situation was tough, and there would be challenges ahead. But now that he had something to strive for, the future seemed bright.

"Well, okay. I'll support you until you see your dream through."

"Thanks. You'll probably need to . . ."

"Sure, I'll pick up some more hours at work."

Somewhat surprised by Yuko's understanding, he bowed his head in appreciation.

"But why soba? You said these are a keepsake from your dad?"

"Well . . ."

Shuichi wasn't quite sure how much to reveal. Knowing no one would believe the driver's story anyway, he kept his answer vague, stating that one curious thing led to another, taking him on a business trip near his hometown where he decided to drop in.

That night, Shuichi wrote his letter of resignation.

ON FRIDAY, THE NEXT DAY, SHUICHI TOOK OFF WORK.

It was the day before the month's closing date, but

since it fell on a Saturday, his month's salary had already been calculated. Ultimately, Shuichi couldn't recover any of the twenty canceled contracts; thus, he decided to take paid leave until payday. Despite the sudden request, Wakiya approved it without a word. Perhaps he sensed that Shuichi was contemplating quitting.

Payday was set for next Thursday, and Shuichi spent Monday through Wednesday attempting to make soba using Masafumi's tools. The result was very different from what could properly be called soba, and the road ahead seemed more difficult than he had anticipated. Despite being disheartened, Shuichi reminded himself that he was only just getting started.

On payday, there was always an all-staff meeting. At the end of the meeting, everyone received their pay slip in an envelope from the company president. When it was his turn to receive his envelope, Shuichi approached Wakiya and asked, "There's something I'd like to discuss with you. Do you have a moment?"

Wakiya, nodding immediately as if he'd expected the request, answered, "I have something to discuss too. Let me make a quick call, and I'll meet you in the reception room in fifteen minutes?"

Shuichi bowed his head.

Returning to his desk, he took out the pay slip from the envelope and checked the amount. Every month, whether the amount had increased or decreased, his heart raced a little examining it. On this day, however, he found himself unusually composed.

Wakiya came into the reception room fifteen minutes later.

Shuichi, who was already seated, stood up to greet him. "Thank you for making time to see me."

Wakiya smiled and waved a hand as if to say don't worry about it. "What is it you wanted to talk to me about?" he asked, taking a seat.

Shuichi followed and sat back down. He took out the resignation letter from inside his jacket pocket and placed it on the table.

"I'd like to resign from the company."

Wakiya remained expressionless as he gazed at the envelope.

Shuichi waited for a response, but when none came, he continued, "The reason is written there, so I think you'll understand after you've read it."

There was an uneasy silence between them as Wakiya continued to stare at the envelope looking none too concerned. His calm demeanor suggested that he may have anticipated Shuichi's resignation. Given the mass cancellations Shuichi had incurred, anyone could have concluded that this moment was inevitable.

Wakiya's gaze shifted from the envelope to Shuichi. The expression on his face was gentle, perhaps even smiling. "Anything else you'd like to say?"

"Thank you for everything. I know I couldn't contribute much, but I appreciate everything you've done for me. I've been clumsy, oddly stubborn, and not very forthright, to say the least. But I've finally started to grasp the meaning behind the words you've imparted. As hardheaded as I am, I'm sure I've caused you trouble."

"Oh? What words, specifically?"

"You often said, 'Stay positive, and laugh more than anyone else.' I wrestled with that idea of positive thinking, so every time I heard it, I kept debating whether it really was that simple to be positive with a snap of a finger. I wasn't honest with myself. However, a certain experience helped me to understand what true positive thinking is. It made me realize that I wasn't incapable of it. Just that I wasn't open enough to accept it."

"What is true positive thinking as you understand it?"

"The way I understand it, positive thinking is about accumulating luck in your lifetime and leaving more luck when you die than . . ."

Suddenly a shock wave surged through his head. Many events flooded back into his mind and connected in a way that seemed almost absurdly persuasive. His heart was racing.

"What is it?" asked Wakiya. "More luck when you die than . . . ?"

"Hang on, do you mind if I ask you something?"

"Ask me what?"

"Last week, when I gave you the Akafuku, you said that you couldn't get enough of them as a kid."

"Yeah?"

"May I ask where you're from originally?"

"I'm from Ise."

Shuichi hesitated for a moment.

"Something the matter?" asked Wakiya.

"I just had a thought. Can I ask you a strange question?"

"What?"

"Your grandfather. What was he like?"

"My grandfather?" Wakiya appeared genuinely puzzled by the question. "He died in the war soon after my father was born, so I couldn't tell you."

"Was he in Saipan?"

Wakiya shot him a look of surprise. "How do you know that?"

"My grandfather was in Saipan too."

"No kidding." Crossing his arms, Wakiya fell into thought.

This time, it was Shuichi who watched Wakiya's

expression change. After a while, Wakiya nearly jumped out of his seat, making Shuichi recoil. "Let me ask you a question."

"Y-yes . . . ?"

"Are you quitting this job . . . to start a soba shop?"

The question astounded Shuichi. "Yes, but . . . how did you know that?"

With a hand on his chin, Wakiya paced the room restlessly, lost in thought. Eventually, he returned to his seat, his expression as calm as usual. "Oh, I just asked is all," he remarked, leaning back casually in his chair. "So, can we move on to what I wanted to discuss?"

"Yes, of course."

"Have you had a chance to look at your pay slip?"

"Yes, I wanted to discuss that with you too. This month's amount was supposed to be considerably less due to the mass cancellations with Saido Seminars, but the amount was more than usual. There must be some kind of mistake."

Shuichi gave an honest report of his salary, which was supposed to be less, not more.

"No, no mistake."

"What do you mean?" Shuichi asked, his face colored with skepticism.

"The business card you gave me. It had Yamamoto-san's cell phone number on it. He was still in Tokyo when I called, so I went to see him."

"Oh?"

"He told me about your meeting. You weren't being straight with me about not being able to close the deal. He said you refused to sign him to a contract yourself and you referred him to me."

Embarrassed, Shuichi forced an uneasy smile. "I . . . had already decided to resign by then, and I wanted to repay you for everything you've done."

"I figured that might be the case. Anyway, I had a talk with him. He was moved by what you had to say about insurance. It seems the very soul of the kind of company he wants to create aligns perfectly with your concept of insurance through mutual assistance.

"His eight restaurants are all staffed with young workers full of energy and dreams, but they don't have any interest in insurance. Yamamoto-san believes having insurance is critical to realizing their dreams of owning restaurants someday. But he's having trouble convincing his young staff of that. That's why he's going to gather his staff and have a financial planner deliver that talk."

"A talk?"

"Yes, and I accepted the offer on your behalf."

"Wait, you're not going to give the talk?"

"How am I supposed to do that when I don't know what you said in the first place? Besides, he specifically asked for you, and I already accepted. You'd be making a liar out of me if you don't go."

"Yes, but . . ." Shuichi scratched his head with a flustered expression. A financial planner? A talk? He had come to discuss his resignation, but after things took an expected turn, he wasn't sure what to do. A million thoughts were racing through his head, but he couldn't make sense of it all. He'd always believed that lectures were given by successful people and, therefore, were something that didn't concern him. So, when the opportunity suddenly came up, it was no wonder he couldn't think straight.

"A failed salesman like me giving a talk?"

"Yamamoto-san is prepared to commit to whatever insurance you recommend. He's also designating you as the primary salesman for his company. If you mean to repay me, even a little, you'd go. Until then . . ." Wakiya picked up the resignation letter that Shuichi had given him. "I'll hold on to this. If you still want to quit afterward, then fine."

Still sensing Shuichi's hesitation, Wakiya continued as if to deliver the decisive blow, "Besides, Yamamoto-san's already paid in advance for the talk."

"You already received payment?" Shuichi's voice cracked in disbelief.

"Yes, and that's why."

"Huh? Why . . . ?"

"Why your salary hasn't gone down. It's because it includes the speaking fee."

"This isn't about whether you're going to continue or quit your job, Okada. This is something only you can do. The speaking fee that we received from Yamamoto-san wasn't something I proposed. He suggested it, hoping that you would be persuaded to share the story you told him with his staff. As a business owner, he believes that having your talk heard by his employees is crucial.

"Do you understand? He didn't propose this to help you. He's asking for your help for the good of the company. It's a role that only you can fulfill. You don't need to impress anyone, and you don't need to think about securing contracts. It's simply that someone found your unvarnished story to be necessary. Just speak your truth. Don't run away from this opportunity."

Still, Shuichi hesitated. He stared at a point on the table, unsure of how to answer or what to do. With no clear answer in sight, he could only keep his silence.

Breaking the silence was Wakiya, who let out a chuckle and muttered, "Why look so glum? You're just being asked to give a talk."

Shuichi let out a barely audible gasp.

If you're not in a good mood, you won't notice a luck-changing opportunity.

The smile of the driver looking back from the front seat floated into his head.

Quickly, Shuichi put on a smile.

"Okay, I'll give it a shot. Thank you," he said, bowing deeply.

Wakiya nodded and said, "Good, then email Yamamoto-san to work out the date and other details with him," then left the reception room.

Alone in the room, Shuichi picked up the business card that Wakiya had left on the table. A smile spread across his face.

INSTEAD OF RETURNING DIRECTLY TO HIS DESK, Wakiya exited the building and stepped out onto the street.

Cars were coming and going on the four-lane street. Wakiya looked to the right. There was a taxi approaching in his direction. He half expected it to stop in front of him, but it passed him by.

Has it been fifteen years already?

Wakiya found his thoughts drifting back to the few days he'd spent with the mysterious taxi driver buried deep in his memory, and he couldn't help but smile.

EPILOGUE

The lunch date with her friends had dragged on, causing Yuko to head home much later than planned. She was supposed to be home by 2:00 p.m. but by the time she reached the train station, it was well past 3:30 p.m. She had worn her new shoes because there wasn't any rain in the forecast, but the sky was now covered in dense clouds, enormous raindrops pounding the asphalt.

"I don't believe this!" Yuko muttered to herself in frustration.

Outside the train station, a long line for a taxi had already formed at the rotary. She had a meeting with Yumeka's homeroom teacher at 4:30, but the wait for the taxi would cause her to miss it. Still, walking home in the rain wasn't an option. Eventually, she stood at the end of the line, hoping that a steady stream of taxis would arrive and waiting for the rain to stop. It was probably a momentary downpour, so if she waited a while, it was likely to let up. But would it stop soon enough?

One hope was that even if she was late, Shuichi might still be able to make it on time. Yuko took out her smartphone and checked Shuichi's location. The blue dot indicated he was somewhere called Saido Seminars. The name sounded familiar. She had a vague memory of Shuichi being ecstatic over securing a slew of contracts over six months ago from a cram school by that name. She tried calling him, but there was no answer. He must be in a meeting. Since his location was quite a bit far from Yumeka's junior high school, she couldn't count on him to arrive on time.

Yuko waited about fifteen minutes for the rain to stop but there was no sign of it letting up. The line had moved only a few meters, and her turn for a taxi wasn't coming anytime soon. But the western sky seemed to be getting slightly brighter, and the sound of the rain pelting against the roof was getting quieter. After concluding she wouldn't make her appointment if she waited any longer, she decided to brave the rain and dash across the street to the convenience store to buy a plastic umbrella. Though she knew her entire lower half would get drenched, she couldn't break the appointment.

"Ugh, I don't believe this. My new shoes!" she grumbled, as she left the line, running beneath as many covered areas as she could. While she waited for the light at the first crosswalk to turn, a taxi pulled up in front of her and opened the rear door. Yuko jumped in without hesitation.

"Miyabi Junior High School, please." She took out a handkerchief from her bag and wiped the raindrops off her hands and clothes, mumbling to herself, "Ugh, just horrible."

Once inside the enclosed space of the vehicle, she noticed the scent of the lavender cream she'd applied on her hands while browsing the department store with her friends intensified with her rising body temperature. She had applied the cream a bit too generously.

The driver responded with a soft "yes," and started the taxi.

Yuko then took out a tissue and wiped the raindrops from her new shoes. When she was done, she leaned back in her seat and heaved an exhausted sigh.

Outside the window, it was sunny. The torrential downpour had passed.

"What is this weather?" Cursing to no one in particular, Yuko took out her cell phone and tried calling Shuichi.

"What is it? I'm working."

The irritation in his voice was palpable. Yuko reacted, too, in irritation.

"You didn't forget, did you? We have a meeting at school today about Yumeka."

"I know, I know, but I'm a little busy right now. I can't just leave in the middle of work."

"Don't you think I know that? If you couldn't

make it, I wish you would have told me, that's all. I can go alone."

Yuko heard him click his tongue.

"Sure, go listen to what they have to say."

"Okay. Oh, and did you send payment for our trip?"

Shuichi faltered for an answer. "Not . . . yet."

"Will you make sure to do it? If we don't pay by next week, our reservation will be canceled."

"Right. By the way . . ."

"Yeah?"

"Nah, it's nothing. Anyway, thanks for going."

She let out a sigh and ended the call.

The driver glanced at Yuko through the mirror. "That was some rain, wasn't it?"

Yuko pushed a smile across her lips. "Yeah, it was horrible."

"But maybe it was better that it happened. After all, you were able to catch this taxi."

"Maybe you're right," she replied, going along with the conversation without thinking too hard about it.

"You don't sound very convinced. Are you aware this taxi is special?"

"Is it?"

"Yes. For starters, you won't be charged for the ride today."

"What? Why?"

"See the meter? It's broken."

Yuko looked at the fare meter. It read 70,020.

She was surprised for a moment, but upon hearing that the ride was free, she was a little relieved. "I guess I'm in luck, then."

"Right? Sure, your new shoes got wet because of the sudden rain, but you were able to catch this taxi. People are inclined to think the worst when something happens, but sometimes it's nice to consider maybe it was better this way."

"Okay . . . but how did you know my shoes are new?"

"People wouldn't normally wipe their shoes over some rain. Only people who happen to be wearing shoes they just bought."

Yuko felt a bit embarrassed when she realized the driver might have overheard her grumbling.

"Life's full of things that you might think are the worst right after they happen, but as time passes and you reflect, you realize that they might have been for the better. So, if you start thinking that it was for the better from the start, lots of things become more enjoyable."

Yuko listened to the driver's words in silence. She felt a bit embarrassed, as if she was being reprimanded for her actions since getting in the taxi, but the driver's tone and overall demeanor were not at all unpleasant. In fact, it was comforting.

"In my line of work, I pick up all sorts of people, and I hear a lot about how something they started out thinking is the worst turns out to be something that leads to their future happiness. For example, there's a story of a certain wife."

The driver began to speak unprompted and continued, "It seems one day, the husband suddenly came home with a rather expensive guitar. What's more, he bought it knowing his salary was about to get cut. The husband was an insurance salesman or something, and his monthly pay depended on his sales performance. Not only that, he practiced the guitar only for a few days before he moved on to a different hobby altogether. Can you guess what it was? It was soba making. Later, because his salary was cut and the premiums from the canceled contracts had to be refunded, the family had to cancel the trip they had planned. The wife was furious and thought everything was horrible."

Just then, the face of her husband floated into Yuko's head. She had been listening to the driver's story as if it were unrelated to her, but as soon as she heard the husband was an insurance salesman, the story suddenly hit much closer to home. Still, she tried to shake off the image of Shuichi playing the guitar. He was the least likely person in the world to look good with a guitar.

"The husband sounds like a handful," she said.

"Right? He forgot all about the guitar and started

making soba at home. Care to guess what happened next?"

"Did he find another hobby?"

The driver shook his head. "It eventually led to a future that turned out for the best."

"What do you mean?"

"The husband started making soba because of something he learned about his family history. As he devoted himself to this pursuit, his lifestyle and values changed, which led to an upturn in sales performance. Many years later, he realized his long-held dream of starting a soba shop with his wife."

"Oh."

"That's when his wife realized the importance of thinking that maybe everything is actually for the better in any situation."

"And the guitar? What happened to the guitar?"

"It turned out that the daughter, who was refusing to go to school at the time, picked up the guitar that her father abandoned and started practicing on it in her room. The parents let her, figuring that it would be better if she had something to do at home rather than nothing. Then, about ten years later, she became a famous musician. Um, what was her name? Gosh, I forgot."

"Wow, who would have thought something like that could happen?"

"Not that it's happened yet."

"What was that?" she asked, unable to pick up what the driver said.

"Oh, it's nothing. We're here."

"Huh? Oh, thank you. Are you sure . . ."

"No payment necessary. Anyway, I've got another passenger waiting."

He seemed to be in a hurry. Yuko hastily got out of the taxi. As soon as the rear door closed, the taxi sped off.

"It's for the better, huh? Maybe it would be good to get Yumeka to start practicing the guitar," she muttered aloud and walked through the gates of the junior high school.

After the rain, the sun was out.

AUTHOR'S NOTE

Completing a single work requires numerous encounters with people and the many experiences and lessons learned from them. This particular work also came together through the accumulation of such encounters and learning experiences. I would like to express my heartfelt gratitude to everyone who contributed to each of these aspects, and especially to Yuji Kinoshita of Heroes Life Company, who provided invaluable assistance in inspiring this work. Thank you very much.

MARCH 1, 2019

YASUSHI KITAGAWA